DD

If Having Eve Around Would Make Things Better, He Could Handle His Feelings—Couldn't He?

As for his unfortunate physical attraction to her…big deal. It wasn't his way to let his feelings cloud his judgment, or his desires dictate his actions. And he certainly wasn't a stranger to deprivation. He'd lived most of his life without the sort of things—such as a home, or family or even a close companion—that other people took for granted. He could handle himself.

As quickly as that, his mind was made up. For Lissy's sake, he'd do it. He'd hire Eve to be her nanny.

And to hell with his gut, which was already warning him that Ms. Chandler was going to be nothing but trouble.

And that he was making a big mistake.

Dear Reader,

Silhouette is celebrating its 20th anniversary throughout 2000! So, to usher in the first summer of the millennium, why not indulge yourself with six powerful, passionate, provocative love stories from Silhouette Desire?

Jackie Merritt returns to Desire with a MAN OF THE MONTH who's *Tough To Tame.* Enjoy the sparks that fly between a rugged ranch manager and the feisty lady who turns his world upside down! Another wonderful romance from RITA Award winner Caroline Cross is in store for you this month with *The Rancher and the Nanny,* in which a rags-to-riches hero learns trust and love from the riches-to-rags woman who cares for his secret child.

Watch for Meagan McKinney's *The Cowboy Meets His Match*—an octogenarian matchmaker sets up an ice-princess heiress with a virile rodeo star. The Desire theme promotion THE BABY BANK, about sperm-bank client heroines who find love unexpectedly, concludes with Susan Crosby's *The Baby Gift.* Wonderful newcomer Sheri WhiteFeather offers another irresistible Native American hero with *Cheyenne Dad.* And Kate Little's hero reunites with his lost love in a marriage of convenience to save her from financial ruin in *The Determined Groom.*

So come join in the celebration and start your summer off on the supersensual side—by reading all six of these tantalizing Desire books!

Enjoy!

Joan Marlow Golan

Joan Marlow Golan
Senior Editor, Silhouette Desire

Please address questions and book requests to:
Silhouette Reader Service
U.S.: 3010 Walden Ave., P.O. Box 1325, Buffalo, NY 14269
Canadian: P.O. Box 609, Fort Erie, Ont. L2A 5X3

The Rancher
and the Nanny
Caroline Cross

Silhouette

Desire

Published by Silhouette Books
America's Publisher of Contemporary Romance

 SILHOUETTE BOOKS

ISBN 0-373-76298-4

THE RANCHER AND THE NANNY

Copyright © 2000 by Jen M. Heaton

Visit Silhouette at www.eHarlequin.com

Printed in U.S.A.

Books by Caroline Cross

Silhouette Desire

Dangerous #810
Rafferty's Angel #851
Truth or Dare #910
Operation Mommy #939
Gavin's Child #1013
The Baby Blizzard #1079
The Notorious Groom #1143
The Paternity Factor #1173
Cinderella's Tycoon #1238
The Rancher and the Nanny #1298

CAROLINE CROSS

always loved to read, but it wasn't until she discovered the romance genre that she felt compelled to write, fascinated by the chance to explore the positive power of love in people's lives. Winner of the prestigious Romance Writers of America's RITA Award for Best Short Contemporary, she's also been thrilled to win the *Romantic Times Magazine* Reviewer's Choice Award for Best Desire, as well as a W.I.S.H. Award. She grew up in central Washington State, attended the University of Puget Sound and now lives outside of Seattle, where she *tries to* work at home despite the chaos created by two telephone-addicted teenage daughters and a husband with a fondness for home-improvement projects. *The Rancher and the Nanny* marks her tenth book for Silhouette. Caroline would love to hear from her readers. She can be reached at P.O. Box 5845, Bellevue, Washington, 98006.

IT'S OUR 20th ANNIVERSARY!
We'll be celebrating all year,
Continuing with these fabulous titles,
On sale in June 2000.

Romance

#1450 Cinderella's Midnight Kiss
Dixie Browning

#1451 Promoted—To Wife!
Raye Morgan

AN OLDER MAN
#1452 Professor and the Nanny
Phyllis Halldorson

The Circle K Sisters
#1453 Never Let You Go
Judy Christenberry

The WEDDING AUCTION
#1454 Contractually His
Myrna Mackenzie

#1455 Just the Husband She Chose
Karen Rose Smith

Desire

MAN OF THE MONTH
#1297 Tough To Tame
Jackie Merritt

#1298 The Rancher and the Nanny
Caroline Cross

MATCHED IN MONTANA
#1299 The Cowboy Meets His Match
Meagan McKinney

#1300 Cheyenne Dad
Sheri WhiteFeather

the Baby Bank
#1301 The Baby Gift
Susan Crosby

#1302 The Determined Groom
Kate Little

Intimate Moments

#1009 The Wildes of Wyoming—Ace
Ruth Langan

#1010 The Best Man
Linda Turner

#1011 Beautiful Stranger
Ruth Wind

#1012 Her Secret Guardian
Sally Tyler Hayes

#1013 Undercover with the Enemy
Christine Michels

#1014 The Lawman's Last Stand
Vickie Taylor

Special Edition

#1327 The Baby Quilt
Christine Flynn

#1328 Irish Rebel
Nora Roberts

#1329 To a MacAllister Born
Joan Elliott Pickart

A Family Bond
#1330 A Man Apart
Ginna Gray

DESERT ROGUES
#1331 The Sheik's Secret Bride
Susan Mallery

#1332 The Price of Honor
Janis Reams Hudson

One

The shiny black pickup rocketed down the Bar M's gravel drive, raising a plume of dust in its wake.

Poised before the ranch house's back door, Eve Chandler turned as the vehicle swept past. Her stomach did a quick somersault at the sight of the big, dark-haired man behind the wheel.

It had been eight years since she last saw John MacLaren, but for an instant time seemed to melt away. All of a sudden she was seventeen again, and the way she'd felt whenever she was around him—hot, bothered, filled with yearnings that both enthralled and embarrassed her—came rushing back.

She shivered and took a step toward the stairs as if to flee, only to freeze a second later as her common sense kicked in.

Knock it off, Eve. You're no longer an inexperienced teenager, remember? You're twenty-five years old, the same age John was all those years ago. At least he doesn't have a clue how you felt back then— you made sure of that. Think how much harder this would be if he had.

The stark reminder of why she was here crashed over her like a breaker of icy water. And though she stubbornly refused to give in to the rising tide of panic that had been building inside her the past few weeks, she couldn't deny the irony of the situation. If someone had tried to tell her six months ago that she, the privileged granddaughter of Lander County's biggest rancher, would soon be forced to come begging favors from the sexy loner who once worked in the Chandler stables, she never would have believed it.

Yet here she was.

Thirty feet away, John pulled in beside the small red car she'd borrowed for the drive over. He switched off the pickup's engine.

She could hear her heart pounding in the ensuing silence. Determined not to let on, she deliberately struck a casual pose as he climbed out of the cab and shut the truck door. He began to walk in her direction, his long legs eating up the distance as he slowly yanked off his leather work gloves.

If he was surprised to see her, it didn't show.

He stopped at the foot of the stairs and inclined his head a scant inch. "Eve."

Taking a firm grip on her unruly emotions, she summoned her most confident smile. "Hello, John."

There was a distinct silence as they regarded each other.

Around them, the September day was much like any other. A pale yellow sun hung high in the vast blue Montana sky. The temperature hovered in the mid-fifties, while the summer-seared grass that covered the surrounding range waved gently beneath a light but persistent breeze.

Eve paid no attention. Her focus was completely claimed by the tall man standing before her. Despite her little pep talk, the fluttery feeling in her stomach got worse as he slowly rocked back on his heels and gave her an unhurried once-over. His gaze touched on her sunny blond hair, then raked her ice-blue cashmere sweater, gray wool crepe slacks and Italian leather shoes.

She'd chosen the expensive outfit deliberately. At the time, she'd told herself she merely wanted to look her best. Now, she realized that on some level she'd also hoped it would give her an edge, acting as a subtle reminder of their respective pasts. In the half second before his eyes hooded over, however, she caught a glimpse of something in their depths that seemed to be as much cool disdain as grudging appreciation.

Stung, she lifted her chin and studied him in turn. She had to concede the years had been good to him in ways that had nothing to do with his newfound wealth. He might be dressed in scuffed cowboy boots, jeans whitened at the hips and thighs, a faded black T-shirt and a weathered Stetson, but nobody would ever mistake him for a simple ranch hand.

Time had added muscle to his lean six-foot three-inch frame and character to the chiseled angles of his face. What's more, while he'd always possessed more than his share of virility, now he also radiated an air of leashed power. It was easy to see why women from sixteen to sixty turned to watch when he walked past. From the determined angle of his square jaw, to the compelling bite of his laser blue eyes and the deliberate set of his broad shoulders, he was all man.

The realization that she found him even more attractive now than she had when she was seventeen set off an alarm deep inside her.

"I was sorry to hear about Max," he said abruptly.

She jerked her gaze to his, heat rising in her cheeks as their eyes met. Horrified he might guess what she'd been thinking, she did her best to look cool and contained. "I received your card. Thank you."

He shrugged, the simple motion seriously straining the seams of his T-shirt. "He was a good man."

Off balance, and unable to think about the unexpected loss of her grandfather without a piercing sense of grief, she said merely, "Yes, he was."

"Rumor has it you're selling the Rocking C to some big Texas cattle consortium."

"That's true, I am. The deal will be final in just a few days."

He crossed his arms. "You sure didn't waste any time unloading the place, did you?"

Eve stared at his hard, handsome face, taken aback by his obvious disapproval even as she realized he'd just given her the perfect opening. All she had to do was tell the truth—that if she hadn't sold out to the Texans, she would have lost the ranch either to the bank or the IRS—and he'd know the gravity of her financial situation.

Yet she couldn't—she wouldn't—do it. Word of the disastrous investments her grandfather had made the last year of his life would no doubt eventually surface, since the Lander County ranching community was surprisingly tight-knit. But it wouldn't come from her. Just as Max Chandler had protected her in life, Eve would protect him in death. Because she'd loved him. And because it was the very least that she owed him.

"I guess that means you'll be taking off pretty soon," John said in the face of her silence. "Back to Paris or New York or—where is it you've been living lately?"

"London," she supplied automatically, trying to decide just how she was going to broach the reason for her visit.

She needn't have worried. In his direct, no-nonsense way, John took care of the problem for her. "So, you going to tell me what you're doing here or not?"

"Yes, of course. I was hoping we could talk. There's something I'd like to discuss with you."

He took a cursory glance at his wristwatch, then shocked her by shaking his head. "Sorry. I've got a prior commitment. We'll have to do it another time."

"But this won't wait!"

He shrugged, clearly unmoved. "It'll have to. I've got less than fifteen minutes before I have to be somewhere."

Struggling for composure, she turned to keep him in view as he strode up the stairs and brushed past her, trailing the scent of sunshine, horses and hard work in his wake. "Please, John," she said, swallowing her pride. "I promise it won't take long."

His hand froze on the doorknob. He turned, obvious reluctance warring with curiosity—and something else she couldn't define—in his eyes. "All right," he said finally. "I guess if you don't mind talking while I get washed up, I can spare you a few minutes." Pushing open the inner door, he disappeared inside.

She stared after him, feeling both relieved and annoyed, trying to convince herself that she shouldn't read too much into his being less than friendly. After all, he was simply treating her the way she'd treated him when they were younger.

And just like that, despite her every intention not to revisit the past, the memory of their first meeting came rushing back.

Once again it was a still summer morning. The air smelled clean and sweet, redolent with the scents of sunshine, hay and the bark chips beneath her feet as she stood in the doorway of one of the Rocking C's roomy box stalls, stroking the warm, satiny neck of Candy Stripes, her quarter horse mare.

The two had just returned from a glorious sunrise ride and Eve vividly remembered how she'd felt at that moment: happy, gloriously alive and totally pleased with her life.

But then, why shouldn't she be? Just seventeen, she was cherished and indulged at home and popular at school, where she was both a cheerleader and an honor student. It wasn't surprising she'd believed the world was hers to order.

And then she'd stepped blithely into the corridor, directly into the path of a big, dark-haired stranger— and everything had changed.

He swore as she smacked into the solid wall of his chest. Yet somehow he still managed to swing the hundred-pound sack of grain he had balanced on one broad shoulder to the ground at the same time he reached out to steady her.

Startled, she'd looked up into the bluest eyes she'd ever seen. And as she took in the rest of his features— the strong cheekbones, the blade-straight nose, the chiseled lips, the silky dark hair tumbling over his brow—something unprecedented happened to her.

Heat pooled between her thighs. Her nipples contracted into stiff, aching points. The starch drained from her knees, and she couldn't seem to remember how to breathe.

For one mad moment she wanted nothing more than to step closer, press her body against his boldly masculine one, bury her face against the pulse beating in the strong column of his throat.

She wanted to touch him and taste him... everywhere. And she wanted it so badly she ached with it.

The discovery shocked her. Confused, frightened, alarmed, she took a hasty step back, jerking away from the steely strength of his warm, calloused hand gripping her arm. "Who are you?" she demanded.

He didn't immediately answer. Instead, he looked her over, taking note of the way she was rubbing her fingers over the spot where his hand had been. His mouth compressed slightly, but when his gaze met hers, it was coolly polite—and nothing more. "John MacLaren."

"What are you doing here?"

"Working."

It was bad enough that her body was still throbbing, her throat dry, her heart pounding. But even worse, *he* seemed completely unaffected. She lifted her chin. "Since when?"

"Since I was hired yesterday. And if you don't mind my asking—" he shifted his weight onto one hip in a way she found both arrogant and enticing "—just who are you to be asking?"

She drew herself up a little straighter. "Eve Chandler. My grandfather owns this place."

"Huh."

He sounded completely unimpressed, and panicked by the storm of unfamiliar emotions roaring through her, she snapped, "And if you want to keep your job, I'd suggest you watch where you're going from now on."

He reached over and carelessly hefted the sack of grain onto his shoulder. "I'll keep that in mind." With that, he'd strode away.

Eve stared after him. At any other time in her life she would have been mortified by her rude behavior. But not at that moment. Not with him. Instead, she'd told herself that John MacLaren was an arrogant bore who wasn't worth her time.

Yet every time she'd seen him from that point forward she'd felt that same overwhelming arousal and attraction. It had embarrassed her, made her feel self-conscious and unsure of herself—a new and unwelcome experience. Worse, she'd lived in constant terror that he might discern how she felt. It was no wonder that she'd decided that it was smarter to invite his dislike than risk having him find out how vulnerable he made her feel.

And since she wasn't about to confess the truth after all these years, she could hardly expect him to fall all over himself, welcoming her, she reminded herself now. She'd simply have to do the best she could.

And try to remember that he was her last hope. That no matter what she felt, she couldn't afford to give up on him now.

She drew herself up and walked toward the door. Entering the house, she found herself standing in a spacious, sun-filled mudroom. She had a quick impression of a granite-tiled floor, of a wall covered with hooks that held coats, hats, chaps and all sorts of other equipment, of an alcove housing an oversize washer and dryer. To her left was even what appeared to be a spacious bathroom equipped with a glassed-in shower.

But it was the sight of John planted before a large utility sink with his back to her that commanded her attention. He'd tossed his hat on a nearby counter and yanked his dusty T-shirt out of his jeans. Now, he tugged the garment over his head and tossed it to the floor.

An unwitting voyeur, Eve stared at his smooth, sun-bronzed back, observing the muscles bunch and shift as he turned on the water, picked up the soap and proceeded to wash. When he bent to rinse off, the satiny hollow of his spine flattened out, exposing a ribbon of taut, pale skin at his belt line.

She was so transfixed that she almost didn't look away in time as he abruptly shut off the water, grabbed a towel and swiveled around. "Well?" He waited expectantly.

She forced herself to meet his gaze, trying to behave as if she wasn't acutely aware of his seminakedness. It wasn't easy to do, particularly when an unwanted ribbon of heat curled through her as he rubbed the towel down his neck and over the sculpted contours of his chest. "I had lunch with Chrissy Abrams last week," she began, ordering herself to concentrate. "She told me that you have a seven-year-old daughter who recently came to live with you. And that you've been trying since summer to find somebody to look after her."

"So?"

"So I'd like the job."

He went absolutely still, and then a faint smile curved his mouth. "You're joking, right?"

"No. No, I'm not."

The smile faded. He gave her a long, penetrating look. "Why would you want to do that?"

She'd known he was bound to ask and she was ready. Keeping her eyes steady on his face, she said with a lightness she didn't feel, "Because Lander is my home. I've missed it and I'd like to stay in the area. And now that I've sold the ranch, I need something to do."

"And you think working for me is it?" His face hardened and he slowly shook his head. "I don't think so, Eve."

Even though she'd suspected it was coming, his answer was crushing. She swallowed. "Why not?"

He tossed the towel onto the counter and headed for the dryer, where he retrieved a clean blue T-shirt several shades lighter than his eyes. Frowning, he peeled off a small white lace-edged sock that clung to it, tossing the stocking onto the washer top. He pulled on the shirt and strolled back toward the sink, stuffing the tail into his jeans as he went. "Let's just say I don't think you're the right woman for the job."

"But I am." She struggled to keep the desperation out of her voice. "I'm here, I'm available, I know my way around a ranch and I'm very, very good with kids."

He leaned back against the counter, looking singularly unconvinced. "Maybe. But it doesn't matter. Chrissy apparently didn't tell you that I need somebody who's willing to live in."

"Actually, she did."

His glorious blue eyes narrowed slightly. "And that's all right with you?"

Clearly now was not the time to admit it was the prospect of living with him that had made her exhaust every possibility of other employment first. "Yes."

"Well, it's not with me. This'll probably come as a shock to you, princess," his voice took on a distinctly sarcastic tone, "but I need somebody who can do more than just keep Lissy company. I don't have either a cook or a maid, so I'm looking for someone who can run a house, too."

She absolutely was *not* going to lose her temper. Still, she couldn't keep the tartness out of her own voice as she answered. "I think I can handle it, John. I know how to cook and clean. More importantly, as I understand it, your daughter's not having the easiest time fitting in at school—" she saw his mouth tighten and knew she was moving into dangerous territory "—and I think I can help."

"Chrissy Abrams talks too much," he said flatly.

"Maybe. But that doesn't change the fact that I have something unique to offer. I was just a little older than your daughter when I lost my parents and came to live with Granddad. I know what it's like to be uprooted, to lose one way of life and make the adjustment to another."

He shook his head. "Even if you have more moves than Mary Poppins, the answer is still no, Eve."

"But—" For one reckless moment she nearly blurted out the truth. *Please. I need this job. I've sold everything of value I can, I've got less than three hundred dollars to my name and in four days I'll be homeless—*

"I'm sorry." John coolly interrupted her frantic thoughts. "But it just wouldn't work."

The finality in his voice was unmistakable. Like a slap in the face, it brought Eve to her senses. A shiver went through her as she realized just how close she'd come to begging for his help and shaming her grandfather's memory.

Even so, she couldn't stop the hot wash of tears that prickled her eyes as her last hope died. She glanced quickly away and blinked hard, swallowing around the sudden lump in her throat. "I see."

It would be all right, she told herself fiercely. This was merely another setback, not the end of the road. Something was bound to turn up. The important thing now was not to make a bigger fool of herself than she already had by coming here.

She swallowed again. Raising her chin, she forced herself to face him. "Well." She managed a smile. "I guess I'm not going to change your mind, am I?"

He shook his head. "No."

She felt her lower lip start to tremble and glanced blindly at her watch. "Then I'd better let you go, or you'll be late."

To her relief, he shifted his gaze to his own wristwatch and she seized the opportunity to turn away. Although she suddenly wanted nothing more than to escape, she forced herself to stroll toward the door. Summoning up another surface smile, she glanced over her shoulder. "It was nice seeing you again, John."

He nodded, his expression impossible to read. "You, too."

"I hope you find someone soon."

"Sure."

And then she was out the door and crossing the porch. She made her way to her car, her steps deliberately measured. Climbing in, she turned the key she'd left in the ignition, backed out carefully and pulled onto the ranch driveway, resisting the urge to speed.

It wasn't until she reached the highway that she could no longer ignore the way her hands were shaking. Tightening her grip on the steering wheel, she pulled over and stopped the car, struggling to yank on the emergency brake as the shaking spread.

Stubbornly, she again tried to tell herself that everything was going to be all right.

Except that deep down, she no longer believed it.

She squeezed her eyes shut, but it was too late. A single tear slid down her face as she wondered what she was going to do now.

Two

The pickup rattled over the cattle guard with a muted thump of its heavy-duty tires.

Slowing the vehicle as he reached the highway, John turned to the left, pulled over onto the shoulder and braked. Squinting into the sun, he looked toward the west and quickly spotted the distinctive yellow school bus still well off in the distance.

He gave a sigh of relief, glad that he wasn't late. Rolling down his window, he switched off the pickup's engine and settled back to wait, aware, as he felt the tension in his shoulders, that he was strung tighter than seven feet of barbwire on an eight-foot section of fence.

He knew exactly who was to blame.

Although he'd promised himself he wasn't going to think about her, his thoughts zeroed in on Eve. You could have knocked him over with a feather when he'd pulled into the yard and seen her. After all these years, she was still as blond and beautiful as ever. Not to mention as self-assured. What was it she'd said about her job qualifications?

Oh, yeah. *I think I have something unique to offer.*

Well, she sure as hell was right about *that.* And for all he knew, she also wasn't half bad when it came to taking care of kids.

His mouth twisted caustically. He wasn't a man to hold a grudge but he wasn't a fool, either. He hadn't forgotten the way she'd acted toward him all those years ago, before she'd left for her fancy college. Slim and long-legged, with golden skin, clear gray eyes and the straightest, whitest teeth he'd ever seen, at seventeen she'd been an absolute charmer—with everyone but him.

Since there had never been anything wrong with his ego, he'd known damn well he wasn't without a certain appeal of his own. For whatever reason—his size, the innate aloofness that gave him an air of being hard to get, the fact that he was an orphan—women had been drawn to him since his early teens.

But not the lovely Ms. Chandler. She'd taken an obvious dislike to him at first sight. There had been no sunny smiles, none of the warmth or practical jokes or wry teasing she bestowed on the rest of the hands. Instead, although always faultlessly polite, she'd treated him as if he smelled bad.

He sure as hell hadn't appreciated her attitude. But he had needed the job, so he'd sucked it in and done his best to ignore her. He'd told himself she was nothing more than a kid. And that she was actually doing him a favor, since he'd known that Max Chandler would fire him in a second if he showed the slightest interest in her.

Still, it had rankled. And for all that he'd never let on, it hadn't been long before he'd itched to take her down a peg and wipe that superior look off her pretty face. Making matters worse, on some level he'd known that the urge sprang not from a need for respect or revenge but because he wanted her. He'd wanted to thrust his hands in her silky blond hair and taste her smooth pink mouth. He'd wanted to feel her slim, golden body under his. He'd wanted to touch her all over and make her cry out his name.

Spoiled or not, she'd made him ache.

Which was all water under the bridge, he reminded himself now. Sure, she still looked damn good, maybe even better than before. And yeah, there was still something about her—the husky timbre of her voice, the graceful way she moved, the silky-soft look of her hair and skin—that seemed to go straight to his groin and play hell with the fit of his jeans. But as for her suggestion that she come to work for him...

John's expression turned cynical. No matter how much he needed the help, or how appealing the thought of being Eve's boss, he had no intention of indulging the whims of the Rocking C's patrician princess.

She was all wrong for the job, for one thing. He needed someone who would take care of practical matters without caring if she mussed her hair. And that someone had to be warm, grounded and nurturing, not a spoiled social butterfly. What's more, she had to be willing to stick around longer than it took for a coat of nail polish to dry.

When it came to Eve, he especially doubted her

staying power. She could talk all she wanted about how she'd missed home and wanted to remain in the area, but he was sure it wouldn't be very long before she changed her mind. After all, what could Lander offer compared to New York or London or Paris? And why would she suddenly feel the need for a job, when she'd spent the past few years as a lady of leisure?

Unless... He shifted, feeling a trace uneasy. He'd heard rumors a few months back that Max Chandler was in financial trouble. At the time, he'd been too preoccupied with the discovery that he had a daughter to pay much attention. When he had bothered to think about it, he'd just assumed the gossips must be wrong. Although rising expenses and a downward trend in the price of cattle had bankrupted a lot of spreads over the past few years, he couldn't believe anyone as shrewd as Max would allow things to get out of hand. And yet, if he had, that might explain Eve's surprising desire for employment.

The sound of squealing brakes interrupted his speculations. Looking up, he saw the school bus had finally arrived. As he watched, the hinged stop sign swung out and the red and yellow warning lights flashed on. With a swoosh of escaping air, the door folded back and Lissy appeared.

John's heart squeezed as he took her in. She was barely bigger than a minute, with her skinny arms, pale little face and big blue eyes. And though her outfit was hardly stylish—he winced a little at the orange sweater, red-plaid skirt that fell to midcalf and the pink frilly socks with the white patent leather mary-janes— he didn't care. She was *his* daughter, his flesh and blood. He felt a rush of emotion—love, awe, tenderness—so strong, it was almost painful.

Not that it mattered, he was quick to remind himself as their gazes met and she sent him a brief, uncertain smile before glancing away. No matter how strongly he felt about being a father, he and his daughter were still strangers. Her mother—a woman he barely remembered—had made sure of that.

John's jaw tightened. He still didn't understand why Elaine hadn't come to him when she found out she was pregnant. Granted, the handful of times they'd spent together had been more a series of one-night stands than an actual affair. And by insisting on using protection, he had made it clear that he wasn't interested in a commitment.

But if she had just sought him out, told him that something had gone wrong and that she was carrying his child, he would have married her in an instant. He was a man who took care of his obligations.

Instead, she'd remained silent, even when she fell ill and left *his* child with her mother to raise. Hell, if the old lady hadn't gotten sick herself, he never would have known he had a kid.

He shook his head. Every time he thought about all the years he'd missed with Lissy, it made him a little crazy. He couldn't help thinking that maybe, if he'd had a chance to get to know her as a baby, to see her grow and get acquainted with her gradually, he wouldn't be such a bust as a parent now.

Then again, maybe not. The truth was, the Lander County Boys' Home hadn't prepared him for fatherhood, instant or otherwise. Nor had it taught him the first thing about being part of a family. No matter how hard he tried, he didn't know what to say or how to act, much less how to befriend a little kid—and a girl, at that.

And though he wasn't surprised, it ate at him. He'd long ago decided he'd never marry, since what he'd seen at the orphanage—boys left alone, whether by their parents' choices or by their parents' deaths—had convinced him that love couldn't be depended upon. But with Lissy it was different, since neither of them had a choice in the matter. She was here, and he was here, and he knew damn well that she deserved better than he was able to give.

Still, they'd managed all right during the summer. Due, no doubt, to the fact that his nearest neighbor's teenage daughter had been willing to baby-sit, leaving him pretty much free to go about his business as usual. Now that school had started and he and Lis were on their own, it wasn't so simple, however. In addition to having a twelve-thousand-acre ranch to run, he had to contend with baths, bedtimes, laundry and meals. And without someone to run interference, his normal reticence combined with his daughter's shyness was making for increasingly long and awkward silences.

Across the way, Lissy started down the bus's steep metal stairs. It was his signal to climb out of the truck, and he did, striding around to the other side as she walked up. "Hey, Lissy." Opening the passenger door, he reached for her bright red backpack and tossed it onto the truck's abbreviated back seat.

She glanced shyly up at him. "Hi."

He reached out and boosted her carefully onto the seat. She weighed next to nothing, making him acutely aware of his own strength. Straightening, he stepped back and waited for her to fasten her seat belt. Once she did, he shut her door, walked around and got in on his own side. As soon as the bus lumbered away, he started the truck, made a tight U-turn and headed back to the ranch.

Silence reigned as he tried to think of something to say. Finally, after more than a mile, he glanced surreptitiously at her. She jerked her gaze away from him and stared down at her lap, pink touching her cheeks as she began to pluck at her skirt with her pale fingers.

He cleared his throat. "So...how was your day?"

She shrugged one thin shoulder. "Okay."

"Anything interesting happen?"

Her fingers stilled. After a moment, she nodded. "Uh-huh."

He waited, but she remained silent. "What?" he said finally.

To his surprise, she suddenly sucked in a breath and turned to face him. "Jenny Handelmen asked me to come to her birthday party!"

He stared at her. Her usually sober little face was lit up like a Christmas tree. "She did?"

"Uh-huh. She wasn't going to—" her pleasure dimmed a fraction "—but her mom said she had to ask all the girls in the class."

John suppressed the urge to ask who in the hell had felt compelled to tell her *that*. "Yeah, well, the important thing is you got invited," he said awkwardly.

She appeared to think about that. "I guess." Her face brightened. "She's going to have pizza, and a Barbie cake and chocolate ice cream. And she said we're gonna play games!"

He frowned, surprised by the extent of her excitement. "That's good, huh?"

She started to reply, then appeared to reconsider. "I think so."

"Don't you know?"

She shook her head and her unruly mop of dark blond corkscrew curls bobbed around her shoulders, making him belatedly wonder what had become of the ponytail he'd struggled so hard to secure that morning. "I—I've never been to a birthday party before."

"You haven't?"

"Uh-uh."

"Why not?"

She shrugged, her expression suddenly uncertain. "Grandma always said no."

"Huh." He'd known Lissy's grandmother only briefly, but it hadn't taken him long to form an opinion about her character. He wondered if it had been disapproval of having fun in general or the price of a gift that had made the old lady deny the kid such a simple pleasure.

"So can I go?"

He started to say yes, then caught himself. "When is it?"

"Saturday."

"This Saturday? Tomorrow?"

"Uh uh." She shook her head. "The next one."

His heart sank. "Are you sure?"

"Uh-huh."

"What time?"

"Six. Remember, I told you, we're gonna have pizza for dinner."

Great. The annual Cattlemen's Association banquet was due to kick off at seven the same night in Missoula, a hundred and twenty-five miles away. He'd already tried and failed to get a sitter, so he'd gone ahead and made a reservation for the two of them at the hotel. As outgoing president, there was no way he could miss it.

Yet something told him that Lissy wasn't going to see it that way. He glanced at her. For once she was staring straight at him. Her eyes—the same intense blue as his own—were bright with anticipation. "Can I go? Please?"

He swallowed a curse. "No, I'm afraid not."

She blinked in surprise, her long lashes brushing her translucent cheeks as all the joy drained from her face. "Oh," she said in a small voice.

"Look, I'm sorry." Even to his own ears, his voice sounded stilted. "I've got a meeting that night and I can't miss it."

"Oh," she said again. She swallowed hard, turning away to once more stare down at her lap. "It's okay," she said after a moment. "I—I didn't really want to go anyway."

It was clearly a lie. Yet try as he might, John couldn't think how to address it—much less what he could say that would make things better. Feeling guilty and frustrated, he looked away from her still little face and pretended to be absorbed in the road in front of him.

They traveled the last half mile to the house in total silence. Pulling into the same spot where he'd parked earlier, he stopped the truck and turned off the engine. "I've got to get some stuff from the barn," he said gruffly. He nodded toward the porch. "Why don't you go on in? Have a quick snack and then you need to change into some play clothes."

"What for?" she said dully.

"We need to run some salt licks up to the herd at Blue Ridge."

She still didn't look at him. "But...couldn't I stay here? Please?"

He considered. It was a good thirty miles to the ridge round-trip. It would be dark by the time he got back. If something were to happen to her... He shook his head. "No."

Silence. And then, with an air of utter dejection, she gave a faint sigh. "Okay." Without another word, she opened the door and climbed out, sliding the last foot to the ground before nudging the door shut and heading for the porch. She looked very small and very much alone as she trudged along, her shoulders slumped, her feet dragging in her scuffed white shoes.

John watched until she disappeared inside the house. For a moment he sat motionless. Then he let loose a curse and slammed his fist against the dashboard. *Damn it!* She deserved better than this. She deserved better than *him.* There had to be something he could do, some way he could make things better—

There is, you sorry sonofabitch. The solution was here earlier asking for a job—remember?

The thought froze him in place. He started to deny it, but in the next moment all his earlier arguments against hiring Eve seemed to fade away, replaced by the image of Lissy's sad little face. He sank back against the seat, his anger abruptly replaced by a sort of grim resignation.

Okay. So he didn't particularly like Eve. What did it matter? It was Lissy's happiness that was important. And it wasn't as if he had other options. If having Eve around would make things better, he could handle his feelings—couldn't he?

As for his unfortunate physical attraction to her... Big deal. It wasn't his way to let his feelings cloud his judgment, or his desires dictate his actions. And he certainly wasn't a stranger to deprivation. He'd lived most of his life without the sort of things—such as a home or family or even a close companion—that other people took for granted. He could handle himself.

As quickly as that, his mind was made up. For Lissy's sake, he'd do it.

And to hell with his gut, which was already warning him that Ms. Chandler was going to be nothing but trouble.

And that he was making a big mistake.

Three

"**Y**ou ready?"

Poised in the open doorway of her childhood home, Eve considered John and his less-than-gracious greeting. He looked very big as he stood backlit by afternoon sunshine, the breeze ruffling the navy T-shirt tucked into his close-fitting jeans.

Very big, very remote—and far from friendly. The old adage "Be careful what you wish for" played through her head. Three days ago she'd been distraught when he'd refused to give her a job.

Now, face-to-face with him again, she felt distraught that he had.

A faint, self-mocking sensation curled through her. Clearly this was the time to remind herself that if not for John's change of heart, she'd be on a Greyhound bus right now bound for who knew where. And that no matter how much she might wish he were a different kind of man—more easygoing, more forthcoming, less attractive, less blatantly male—she owed him for giving her a chance.

"Yes," she said pleasantly. "I'm ready. And I really appreciate you coming to get me."

"No problem. That your stuff?" With a jerk of his chin, he indicated the matched set of luggage and the large cardboard box lined up on the porch to his left.

She nodded. "Yes."

Without another word he walked over, picked up a suitcase in either hand and headed for his truck.

Eve watched him stride away, telling herself that he was doing her a favor with his brusque, businesslike manner. Because, for reasons she was sure were solely attributable to some obscure facet of male-female chemistry, she had to admit that after all these years simply looking at him still made her a little breathless. She didn't want to think how she'd react if he ever displayed the least bit of charm.

Not that there appeared to be any chance of that. For which she was extremely grateful, she told herself firmly, forcing herself to look away from his retreating back. She needed this job. It would be the height of folly to let some juvenile attraction get in the way.

It was just hard to remember when John's presence was so unsettling. But then, she supposed in a way she owed him for *that,* too, since her extreme awareness of him seemed to overshadow everything, even her imminent departure from her childhood home.

She turned and took one last look at the familiar entry, the broad staircase, the living room that was never used, the long hall that led to the family room that was.

It had been a good place to grow up. Yet she wasn't

sorry to leave. Being here alone the past few weeks had made her realize that without her grandfather, the ranch was no longer her home.

She settled the strap of her purse on her shoulder and smoothed her suede vest into place over her white, open-neck shirt and slim-fitting jeans. Then she calmly pushed in the lock and stepped outside, pulling the door shut behind her. She was just in time as John came up the stairs again.

He nodded at the single remaining suitcase as he reached for the cardboard box. "You think you could grab that?" He straightened without any sign of strain, although Eve knew how heavy the box was since she'd needed help carrying it outside.

"Of course."

"Then let's go. I need to pick up Lissy and get back to work." He turned on his heel and headed back the way he'd come.

All right. So maybe he was making it difficult to be grateful. She still wasn't going to let him get to her. Chin up, she set out after him, approaching just as he finished setting the box in the bed of the truck. He turned but didn't say anything, merely reached for the suitcase. In the second before it occurred to her to let go, his hand pressed firmly against hers.

It was big, hard and warm, and Eve felt the contact clear to her toes. Startled, she jerked away, her gaze shooting to John's face as she wondered if he'd felt it, too.

If he had, it didn't show. His glorious blue eyes were hooded, his strong, masculine face expressionless as he gazed down at her. With a faint shock, she realized how close he was. Despite the breeze, she could feel the heat roll off of him, carrying with it the faint scent of soap and sweat. And she could see the beard that shadowed his smoothly shaven cheeks, as well as the faint lines that bracketed each side of his chiseled mouth.

Her own mouth suddenly felt desert dry. And still she continued to stare at him, riveted by the sensual curve of his lips—

He abruptly turned away, tossing the bag in the truck with a thump. Leaning over, he snagged an elastic cross tie and secured it across her belongings. Then he straightened, walked the few feet to the passenger door and jerked it open. Leveling a blue-eyed stare at her, he rocked back on his heels. "You getting in or not?"

Eve sucked in a breath. *Remember. You can handle this—no matter how he behaves.* "Of course." Deliberately taking her time, she strolled over and climbed unhurriedly into the cab. Looking out at John, she smiled her most gracious smile. "Thank you."

"Sure." He slammed the door, walked around and climbed in on the driver's side. Neither of them spoke as he started the truck and put it in gear.

Eve stared fixedly outside, watching the familiar landscape roll by. The sky was a vast expanse of cloudless blue that seemed to go on forever. On the far horizon, the mountains rose in shades of gray and plum, their jagged peaks frosted with snow. Closer in, a few head of cattle grazed, all that was left of the once vast Chandler herd.

Regret rocked through her. It came despite her confidence that the ranch would prosper again; the Texas consortium that had bought it had deep pockets and a good reputation. Nor did it seem to matter that in addition to making one year's guaranteed employment for the handful of loyal hands who'd opted to stay on a condition of the sale, she'd also seen to it that they received every dime of their back pay, the best she could do under the circumstances.

She just wished she knew what had prompted her grandfather to make that first risky investment. Or why, when things started to go sour, he hadn't simply accepted his losses instead of stubbornly throwing good money after bad.

She swallowed a sigh. If only she'd paid more attention, instead of blithely assuming that everything was all right. If only she'd come home last spring, instead of letting Granddad convince her the timing was bad. If only she'd behaved more responsibly, he might have felt he could confide in her, instead of believing he had to protect her the way he always had.

"Why didn't you tell me you were broke? That you had to sell the ranch?" John asked abruptly.

The question caught her off-guard. Her stomach twisted even as she gamely raised her chin. "Whatever makes you think that?"

"Don't try to snow me, Eve. I'd already heard some rumors. After you gave me that story about needing a ride today because you were 'between cars,' I got to thinking. I called Eldon Taylor and he filled me in."

Eldon Taylor was the president of Lander Savings and Loan. Eve had never particularly liked him, but until now she'd always thought he was discreet. "He had no right," she said woodenly.

"Maybe not. But the point is, he did." They rattled over the last cattle guard, then drove beneath the carved wooden arch that marked the ranch entrance. After checking for other traffic, John pulled out on the sparsely traveled two-lane highway and accelerated. "And you still haven't answered my question."

"Unlike Mr. Taylor, I didn't think it was any of your business," she said coolly. "I don't recall asking you for a loan. Or a handout." She glanced challengingly at him. "Or do you make everyone who works for you fill out a financial statement?"

A muscle flexed in his jaw. "I'm not entrusting 'everyone' with my daughter. I'm entrusting you. I think that entitles me to ask a few questions."

As much as it rankled, Eve had to concede he had a point. "All right. What is it you want to know?"

"I thought you had a trust fund, money that came from your parents."

"That's right."

"What happened? You blow through it already?"

Before, she'd only suspected he thought she was a spoiled brat. Now she knew. Yet she was darned if she'd defend herself. Not now, and not to him. She shrugged. "As a matter of fact, I did. But don't worry. I swear I won't steal your silver or anything. I'm not that desperate. Yet."

To her satisfaction, his mouth tightened.

Deciding to press her advantage, she added, "What made you change your mind about hiring me, anyway?"

One shoulder rose and fell dismissively. "I don't have time to run the ranch and also take care of a kid. Once I thought about it, I decided that any help was better than none. Even yours."

It was hardly a ringing endorsement, but Eve told herself she didn't care. His opinion wasn't the one that mattered. "What about your daughter? What does she have to say about this?"

He shrugged again. "I've got a meeting in Missoula this Saturday, the same time that one of her classmates is having a birthday party. Your being here means she can go, so I'd say she's for it." He paused, then added almost defensively, "She's not a real big talker."

Eve stared at him in surprise, suddenly wondering if there was something he wasn't telling her. Pursing her lips, she tried to decide how to broach the subject, when suddenly his whole big body stiffened.

"Damn," he said fiercely.

"What's the matter?"

"The bus must've been early."

A quick look around made her realize they were coming up on the entrance for the Bar M. But it wasn't until she followed his gaze that she noticed the forlorn little figure who stood half-hidden next to a large metal mailbox boldly marked MacLaren.

Eve wasn't sure what she'd expected, but it wasn't this.

John's daughter was small and pale, with big blue eyes set in a delicate face and a wild tangle of butterscotch curls that spilled from a bedraggled, off-center ponytail. She was also atrociously dressed in a pea-green nylon slicker, a too-big canary-yellow dress that sported an oversize Peter Pan collar, and a pair of sagging navy kneesocks.

Yet what captured Eve's attention was the way the child took several spontaneous steps forward when she saw the truck, then stopped, as if uncertain of her reception. She hesitated, then raised her hand in a tentative wave.

The vulnerability of the gesture tugged at Eve's heart.

She glanced at John as he pulled over onto the

verge. His face was granite hard as he slammed the transmission into park. He was out the door almost before the pickup had come to a full stop. Yet for all his urgency, he stopped several feet short of his daughter, and he made no attempt to touch her. "You okay?" Although his back was to Eve, his gruff voice carried clearly on the breeze.

The little girl nodded.

"Sorry I'm late."

"It's okay. I just…I thought you forgot."

There was a moment's silence. When he spoke, his voice was even more clipped than before. "I wouldn't do that." He reached down and picked up the small backpack that was lying on the dusty ground. "Come on." He straightened. "There's someone I want you to meet."

The child glanced toward the truck, apprehension suddenly filling her face. "Is that her? Is that the lady who's going to stay with me?" she asked anxiously.

Eve had heard enough. Propelled by an instinct she didn't question, she unlatched her seat belt, scrambled out of the truck and walked over to where father and daughter stood.

Ignoring John, she looked down at the child standing silently at his side. She smiled her most reassuring smile and waited.

There was a brief silence. Then, with an abruptness she pretended not to notice, John said gruffly, "This is my daughter, Lissy." He touched his hand to the child's shoulder. "Lissy, say hello to Miss Chandler."

The little girl looked soberly up at her. "Hello."

"I'm so glad to finally meet you, Lissy," she said warmly. "You can call me Eve, okay?"

The child hesitated, then nodded.

Eve's smile softened. Gently, she reached out and gave Lissy's shoulder a reassuring squeeze. "Good. I just know we're going to be friends."

For a second the child appeared startled. "You do?"

Eve nodded. "Uh-huh. And that's good because I could use a new friend."

"Oh." Lissy hesitated. Her big blue eyes seemed to search Eve's face, and then an uncertain smile trembled across her mouth. "Me, too."

In that moment, Eve lost her heart.

John's house was beautiful as well as functional.

Designed to conform to the surrounding land, the spacious, sprawling, single-story structure was shaped like a trio of rectangles stacked in a sideways stair step. The first block contained the mudroom, which Eve had already seen, and an airy, modern kitchen. A granite-topped eating bar angled along its far side and was open to the second, largest block, which held John's study and a great room. The third block housed the sleeping quarters, with the master bed and bath occupying half the space, three smaller bedrooms and two bathrooms sharing the rest.

Standing in the great room, midway between the kitchen, dining and living areas, Eve admired the huge stone fireplace and the open beams that arched across the vaulted ceiling. The far end of the room jutted out like the bow of a ship and was ribbed with tall windows, so that it seemed to blend with the vast sweep of land and sky outside. The effect was expansive and restful, a feeling echoed by the furniture that was simply but beautifully done using warm woods and soft fabrics in shades of camel, taupe, sand and blue.

"This is wonderful," she said sincerely as John appeared from delivering the last of her things to her room.

He shrugged. "It'll do."

Their gazes met. To her dismay, although he looked about as friendly as an iceberg, she felt a subtle but unrelenting tug of attraction similar to an ocean undertow.

"Where's Lissy?" he said abruptly.

"She went to change her clothes."

"Ah." He considered her for a moment, then headed for the kitchen. "There are some things we need to go over."

"All right." She turned as he walked past her and followed him as far as the eating bar.

Opening the door to the walk-in pantry, he took a set of keys off a hook on the wall. He shut the door, walked over and slid them across the counter to her. "I had the ranch Jeep brought in for you. It's not much to look at, but the engine and the tires are sound and the gas tank's full."

"Thank you."

A faint, slightly cynical smile touched his mouth. "Trust me, it's no Mercedes, princess. But it's safe and it'll get you and Lissy where you need to go."

She inclined her head, since there didn't seem to be anything to say to that.

"We can go over the school bus schedule and any questions you have later. Right now, all you need to know is that the freezer here is fully stocked—" he touched the stainless-steel front of the Sub-Zero next to the matching refrigerator "—and that I'd like to eat by six."

Before Eve could respond, the sound came of somebody knocking at the back door. John strode over to look into the mudroom, then turned back to her. "Sorry," he said, not sounding sorry at all. "That's my foreman. I'd better go see what he wants."

"No problem." She watched him walk away—until it dawned on her that she was admiring the way his jeans clung to his narrow hips and long legs.

Heat climbed into her cheeks. She turned away, wondering a little wildly what it was going to take to dim her awareness of him, only to realize she was pretty sure she wouldn't like the answer.

Irritated with herself, she set off to find Lissy, determined to put John, and her unfortunate reaction to him, out of her mind. Walking quickly down the hallway that fronted the bedrooms, she stopped at what she hoped was the correct door and glanced in.

Like her own room, this one was bright and spacious, with a large closet on one wall and a trio of arch-top windows opposite the door. Yet except for a battered stuffed rabbit propped on the bed, it also felt rather impersonal, like a nicely appointed hotel room. While the carved oak dresser, highboy and double bed with its blue, beige and white bedspread were lovely, they seemed far too old for a seven-year-old.

She spotted her charge lying on her stomach on a blue-and-white braided rug beneath the windows. Several sheets of paper were spread out around her, and a big box of crayons was tipped on its side by her right hand.

Eve knocked, staying put until the child looked up. "Hi. Can I come in?"

Lissy nodded and scrambled into a sitting position.

"What are you up to? Coloring?"

The child nodded again, her face registering near-comical surprise when Eve crossed the rug and sank onto the floor beside her.

"Is it all right for me to look?"

The little girl dropped her gaze, suddenly shy. "Okay."

Eve studied the drawings spread out before her. One was of a tall man with dark hair—clearly John—who stood so much larger than life that he dwarfed the mountain behind him. Another was of an eagle soaring across the sky. And the third, the one that Lissy was obviously working on now, was of a house at night, bright yellow light pouring from the windows beneath a star-spangled sky. Tellingly, there was a dark-haired man framed in one window and a little blond girl in another, both quite alone.

Eve's heart clenched, even as she managed a cheery smile. "These are lovely. Did you know, my friend Chrissy is the sister of your teacher, Miss Abrams?"

"She is?"

"Uh-huh. And I understand that Miss Abrams thinks you're one of the very best artists in her class. I can see why. You draw wonderful pictures."

"Oh." The little girl's face filled with surprised pleasure. "I like to color." She glanced down self-consciously at her lap.

Eve considered that small, bowed head. In addition to her comments about the child's artistic talent, Pam Abrams had also reportedly said that John's daughter could use a woman in her life. At the time, Eve had just assumed—foolishly, she now admitted—that the child must be a miniature version of her father, and what she needed was a civilizing influence.

It didn't take a genius to realize she'd missed the mark. Or to discern that in sharp contrast to her self-assured, self-possessed father, what Lissy was most in need of was someone to give her their undivided attention, to build her up, to boost her confidence and be her champion.

That—and a fashion makeover. Eve swallowed a wry grimace. Just as she'd told John, the youngster had indeed changed out of her school clothes. Now, instead of that awful yellow dress, she was wearing a drab red sweatshirt that sagged at the neck and fell nearly to her knees over a faded, too-short pair of faded pink leggings. The latter exposed her bony little ankles, which protruded above a pair of ruffled lavender anklets and worn white mary-janes.

Eve wondered what on earth John was thinking to allow his child to go around looking like a pint-size bag lady. For someone so prickly proud, it seemed out of character. Then again, she didn't really know him, a fact that was becoming increasingly clear with every hour that passed.

"Oh, I almost forgot. I have something for you."

The child's eyes widened. "You do?"

"Yes, I do." She reached into her vest pocket, pulled out a small, gift-wrapped package and handed it to Lissy. "It's something my granddad gave me when I came to live with him," she said softly, watching as the child carefully began to remove the pink and gold paper. "I thought, since you just recently came to live with your dad, that you might like to have it."

Lissy stared down at the small, velvet gift box she'd unwrapped. Chewing her lower lip in concentration, she pried up the top. "Ohhh!"

Lying on a bed of midnight satin was a small gold

horse pendant, threaded onto a sturdy but pretty gold chain.

Lissy looked at her, her eyes as round as pennies. "Oh, it's so pretty," she breathed.

Eve smiled. "Would you like to try it on?"

The child nodded. "Yes, please."

Eve picked up the necklace, opened the clasp and leaned forward. "Max, my granddad, told me—" she fastened the chain around the child's delicate neck, then sat back to admire the effect "—that wearing this makes you an official Montana cowgirl."

Lissy touched her hand to the necklace. "It does?"

"Absolutely."

"Even…even if you're afraid of horses?"

Eve considered the sudden hope on that little face and added *teach to ride* and *revamp wardrobe* to her quickly growing list of things to do. "Even then," she said firmly, rewarded by one of Lissy's shy, tremulous smiles.

She smiled back, then looked up as an inexplicable little tingle warned her they were no longer alone. Tall and imposing, John stood silently in the doorway. Their gazes met and to her shock, for the briefest moment she could have sworn there was something in his eyes that was dark and hungry.

As if she were seventeen again, her body responded instantly. Her breath caught, her skin flushed, her nipples beaded. Worse, she felt an overwhelming urge to climb to her feet, close the distance between them and indulge herself in the luxury of exploring that big, hard body—

"Look what Eve gave me!"

Lissy's awe-filled exclamation jerked John's gaze toward his daughter. As if released from a spell, Eve snapped back to reality. What on earth had just happened? she wondered, a shiver shuddering through her.

Whatever it was, Lissy thankfully seemed oblivious. Climbing to her feet, the child approached her father and shyly held up the pendant. "See?"

John looked from the necklace to his daughter's upturned face. "It's real nice," he murmured.

The little girl smiled with surprised pleasure and his own expression seemed to lighten fractionally.

He straightened. "I've got to get back to work but I shouldn't be too long." His blue eyes once again found Eve. They were cool and polite, nothing more. "Like I said before, I'd like to eat around six."

"Fine."

"If you need anything, my cell phone number's posted next to the telephone in the kitchen."

She forced herself to smile. "Don't worry about us. We'll manage, won't we, Lissy?"

The child's head bobbed. "Uh-huh."

"All right, then." With a brusque nod, he turned on his heel and left.

It wasn't very mature of her, but in light of her inability to control her rampaging hormones, Eve was glad to see him go.

Four

Eve was seated at the kitchen counter when John walked out of his bedroom Friday morning.

His step faltered as his gaze raked over her, taking note of the slender line of her back, the taut curve of her fanny, the bare feet he could see propped on the bottom rung of the bar stool. With her shining blond hair and sun-kissed skin, she looked all-American exotic, as if she ought to be hanging ten on a beach somewhere.

Not that he gave a damn. Shoving his shirttail into his jeans, he told himself that the sudden tension humming through him was nothing more than annoyance. Growing up at the orphanage, privacy had been non-existent; in the years since he'd left it, he'd come to treasure his morning solitude.

Somehow he doubted Eve would understand, however. With her upbringing, she probably believed he'd be thrilled to see her. God knew, she hadn't held back from making her presence felt in the brief time that she'd been here. Small reminders of her were all over his house, from the bouquet of fall flowers in the center of the dining room table, to the flimsy Italian leather shoes lined up next to his boots in the mudroom, to the faint scent of her perfume that seemed to linger long after she'd left a room.

Still, he was willing to concede that so far she was managing a lot better than he'd expected. The house was clean and tidy. Dinner the past four nights had been delicious. Most importantly, she seemed to really be making an effort with Lissy.

And that was the only thing that mattered.

He crossed the room, his stride firm and purposeful as he walked around the end of the eating counter.

"Good morning," Eve said softly.

Her husky voice tickled along his spine. Deliberately taking his time, he poured himself a cup of coffee before he finally turned to face her. "What are you doing up so early?"

If she was taken aback by the curt question, it didn't show. "I've always been a morning person."

His opinion of that must have shown on his face because the corners of her mouth unexpectedly quirked up.

"I realize it doesn't fit my indolent image—" that tempting mouth curved a little more "—or square with the fact that I slept in the past few mornings, but it's true."

John stared at her. He could see that she'd already showered; her pale hair was still slightly damp. He could also smell her, a faint scent like raindrops on clean, warm skin. But it was the unexpected display of charm that gave him pause—it was as warm and seductive as the first sunny day after a hard winter.

It was also a first where he was concerned and something stirred inside him.

"Besides," she added, her manner abruptly sobering, as if she'd suddenly remembered just who she was addressing, "I also wanted to talk to you."

Ah, that was more like it. Leaning back against the counter, he tried to decide what her problem was likely to be. Would she announce that her bedroom was not up to her standards? Or admit that she'd prefer not to share a bathroom with a seven-year-old? Or would she complain that driving his old Jeep was beneath her? He set down his mug and crossed his arms. "So talk."

"Well, to start with, I have plans to go into town today. I thought I'd better let you know, since dinner may run a little late."

He should have known. "What's the matter, princess? Bored already?"

Her hand froze in the process of raising her coffee mug to her lips. She regarded him for a moment, then slowly shook her head. "No." She took a sip and gently set her cup down on the counter. "On the contrary. I've volunteered to work a few hours a week in Lissy's classroom and I thought I'd start today."

It was so far from what John had expected, it took him a moment to take it in. "You what?"

"I volunteered to—"

He silenced her with a curt wave of his hand. "What I meant was *why*."

"Why what?"

"Why would you do that?"

She began to look a little exasperated. "Oh, I don't know. Maybe because I hope it will make Lissy feel sort of special. And maybe because I hope that feeling special will give her a little added confidence.''

Out of nowhere, a memory flashed through his head. He'd been six years old and in Miss Wakin's first-grade class, and it had been his birthday. He'd waited all day, secretly hoping someone from the Home would show up with cupcakes the way the other kids' moms always did. When nobody had, he'd finally accepted that being an orphan meant no one really cared about you.

He shoved the recollection away, wondering blackly what was wrong with him. This was about Lissy, not him. And no matter his feelings about Eve, he had to concede she had a point. "All right. What else?"

"Excuse me?"

"You kicked off this little discussion by saying, 'to start with.' What else have you got planned?"

Her chin came up a fraction. "Not much. I thought we'd pick up a gift for the birthday party tomorrow. And I also thought we might do some shopping. Not only does Lissy need a dress to wear to the party but her wardrobe could use updating. That is, if it's all right with you."

Despite her impeccably polite tone, there was no mistaking the glint in her clear gray eyes. And though he returned her stare with a steady one of his own, everything that was male in him rose to that unspoken challenge. As the seconds ticked past, he grew increasingly aware of the touch of pink high on her cheeks and the accelerated pulse beating at the base of her throat.

A coil of heat twisted through him. Out of nowhere, he found himself wondering what would happen if he thrust his hands into her pale silky hair, hauled her across the counter and sampled that soft pink mouth with his own.

The thought set off an insistent throb in his groin.

And an alarm in his head. For the second time in under two minutes, he wondered what in the hell his problem was.

But he knew. It was her. Eve. There was just something about her that made him want to cut loose and indulge his baser instincts without a thought to the consequences.

Or would, if he was stupid enough to give in to it.

Which he wasn't. He slapped his coffee cup down on the counter. "Get whatever you think Lis needs. You can sign for it—I've got an account at pretty much every store in town. And don't worry about dinner." He yanked his wallet out of his back pocket, peeled two twenties free and slapped them down on the counter. "As long as you're there, you might as well eat in town."

She looked from the money to him, a slight frown marring her patrician features. "All right," she said slowly. "That's very nice of you."

"Oh, I'm not being nice, princess. I'm just looking forward to some time to myself."

Once more their gazes locked. And though he tried to deny it, for an instant he again felt that unholy desire to wrap his hands in that silky hair, to run his lips over that satiny skin.

By sheer strength of will he forced it away.

Yet as he picked up his car keys off the counter and headed out to work, he found himself thinking it was a damn good thing he was spending the weekend in Missoula.

* * *

"Eve?" Lissy pursed her lips in concentration as she tugged a ruby red tulle skirt into place around Very Velvet Barbie's impossibly slender waist.

"Hmm?"

"Do you think Jenny really likes the present I got her?"

Seated across from the child on the floor, her back propped against one of the great room's oversize club chairs, Eve looked up from the cookbook she'd been perusing. So far she'd done all right, but she could already see that cooking five or six nights a week was going to put a severe strain on her limited culinary repertoire. Hence the cookbook and the pad of sticky notes in her lap. "Sweetie, she loved it. I heard her tell you that myself when I came to pick you up. Between you and me—" she leaned forward and dropped her voice to a confidential whisper "—I'm pretty sure it was her favorite."

The child still didn't look entirely convinced. "You really think so?"

"Absolutely. She got lots of Barbie dolls and stuffed animals, but only one sequined cape and rhinestone tiara."

Lissy considered, then gave a relieved sigh. "Yeah. You're right. All the other girls wanted to try them on. And Jenny did say she likes to play dress-up."

Eve swallowed a fond smile and went back to her cookbook. The past week had taught her that due to her sensitive nature, Lissy was a worrier. Yet she'd also found that with just a little gentle encouragement, the child's natural optimism eventually surfaced.

"Eve?"

"Hmm?"

"Are you sure it'll be okay with my dad for Jenny to come play tomorrow?"

"Of course. Why wouldn't it be?"

A slight frown crinkled Lissy's brow as she picked up a miniature pink comb and began to smooth Barbie's bangs. She gave a little shrug. "Well, my grandma always said that other kids were too loud to have around. She said all that chatter hurt her head."

Eve felt a familiar twinge of dismay. By now she had a pretty clear picture of Lissy's life with her grandmother and it wasn't pretty. As far as she could tell, the elderly lady had believed that children should neither be heard nor seen—and she'd made sure her granddaughter behaved appropriately.

According to Grandma, good little girls played quietly alone in their bedrooms. They didn't wear jeans or laugh too loud or get dirty. They always wore dresses to school, they didn't speak unless spoken to and they never, ever talked back.

Apparently, playmates were also on the forbidden list.

Until now. Just as she'd been doing each time she got the opportunity, Eve tried to reassure Lissy that the rules had changed. "I'm sure your dad won't object."

"Even when he finds out Jenny is going to stay for dinner?"

"Even then. He'll be pleased. You'll see," she said, crossing her fingers that she was right.

On the one hand, John really seemed to care about his daughter. There was just something in his voice whenever he said her name, as well as a subtle gentling in his manner whenever he dealt with her, that made Eve believe his feelings ran deep.

But then again, she could hardly forget the way Lissy had deflated like a punctured balloon when they'd gotten back from shopping Friday night and found the house empty except for a note from John saying he'd decided to go to Missoula a day early.

The child's disappointment had been painful to see, and Eve had been left to wonder whether John didn't know how much he meant to his daughter—or just didn't care.

Frowning, Lissy struggled to force a minuscule Lucite high heel onto one of Barbie's feet. "You're still going to ask him about the horse, aren't you?"

"Sweetie, I told you I would."

"But you promise not to tell him it's for me?"

"That's right." The little girl had been both thrilled and apprehensive when offered the chance to learn to ride. She'd immediately said yes—as long as it could be kept a secret from her father. Eve had reluctantly agreed once she'd realized that Lissy was afraid she might fail and disappoint him.

Barbie's shoe slid on. Lissy reached for the other, but before she could pick it up a flash of sunlight on metal sliced through the room and they both looked over to see John's black pickup roll by the far window.

The little girl's face lit up. "My dad's home!"

"Yes, it sure looks that way," Eve murmured. She tried to tell herself that the sudden kick of her pulse was merely a reaction to the child's excitement, but on some level she knew better.

It was anticipation, pure and simple.

In what seemed no time at all, she heard the back door open and close. Moments later, John strode into the room.

Eve tried not to stare—and failed. Dressed in charcoal slacks and a dove-gray linen shirt, with black boots and a dressy black cowboy hat, he looked heartbreaker handsome. And almost civilized.

Lissy jumped up, her Barbie forgotten. "Hi!" Her voice squeaked with sudden nervousness.

John didn't appear to notice. "Hey, Lissy." For a long moment his gaze lingered on his daughter's face. Then, almost reluctantly, he glanced over at Eve and inclined his head.

Although his expression was as impossible to read as ever, as their gazes met she felt the familiar jolt of his appeal. Only this time she was ready. Taking refuge in action, she climbed to her feet, using the time to compose herself. "Welcome back," she said evenly.

To her relief, he seemed completely unaware of his effect on her. "Thanks." He set his overnight bag on the floor and draped his suitbag over the counter.

"How was your meeting?"

He began to rifle through the previous day's mail. "Good. What about you? Everything go okay?" He didn't bother to look up.

"Everything went fine." She glanced at Lissy; the child was staring intently at him, managing to look both eager and uncertain all at the same time.

Setting the mail aside, he began to sort through his phone messages. A good half minute passed before he finally seemed to become aware of the expectant quality of the silence. He raised his head, a slight frown forming between his brows when he found both Eve and Lissy looking at him.

The silence stretched out until finally Eve couldn't take any more. "I bet you're wondering about the birthday party," she said mildly, trying not to be too obvious.

His expression abruptly cleared. "Yeah. Of course. I was just getting ready to ask." He folded the paper with his phone messages, slipped it into his pocket and turned fractionally toward Lissy. "So—how was it?"

Shyness suddenly tongue-tied the little girl. Digging one small, sneaker-covered toe into the carpet, Lissy gave a little shrug. "Fine."

He frowned. "Did you have fun?"

"Uh-huh."

His voice abruptly softened. "Well, that's good. I'm glad."

It was all the encouragement she needed. Raising her head, she blurted, "Jenny really, really liked the present I got her and her cake had three layers and Barbie on it and I got to wear a party hat and blow a make-noiser and we played pin the tail on the donkey and musical chairs and drop the clothespin and I won at musical chairs and I got this for a prize." Sucking in a much-needed breath, she reached up and touched the pink plastic headband holding back her burnished curls.

"Huh." To Eve's surprise, he didn't seem quite certain how to respond.

"Isn't it pretty?"

"Yeah."

They both fell silent. After a moment, he reached for his bag.

Lissy's face fell.

The next thing she knew, Eve heard herself saying, "She really did have a wonderful time. As a matter of fact, she had so much fun I hated to see it end, so

I invited Jenny to come home with Lissy tomorrow after school and stay for dinner. Isn't that nice?''

John straightened, the bag temporarily forgotten, and stared at her consideringly. ''Yeah. Sure.''

''Then it's okay?'' Lissy said hopefully.

To Eve's relief, he shifted his gaze back to his daughter. ''Sure,'' he repeated.

''Oh, good.'' A happy smile bloomed on Lissy's face.

The sight seemed to give him pause. He appeared to weigh his words, then said carefully, ''You look different today.''

Her smile got even brighter. ''That's 'cause I'm wearing jeans. See?'' With endearing awkwardness, she did a quick pirouette to show him. ''I know they're pink, and they got lace and stuff—'' scrunching up her face, she looked down at the delicate trim that edged the front pockets ''—but Eve says that's okay. They're still jeans.''

''Ah,'' he murmured neutrally.

''And I got my hair cut, too. This much.'' She held up her hands and marked off eight inches, twice as much as had actually been lopped off. ''Now it doesn't get so tangled. And I got lots and lots of other new clothes, too. You want to see?''

He hesitated—and in the next instant the telephone rang. For a moment the sound seemed to freeze him in place, and then with a gesture to Lissy to wait, he walked over and picked up the receiver.

''MacLaren.'' He listened intently for a good thirty seconds before obvious satisfaction flashed across his face. ''Of course my offer still stands, Marty. If you're really willing to part with those heifers, I'm definitely in the market to buy. Let me change phones, and we can go over the figures.''

Punching in the hold button, he glanced at Lissy. ''I'm sorry,'' he said to his daughter, as he replaced the receiver in the cradle and walked around the counter, ''but I really need to take care of this.''

''Oh.'' Her voice, so animated only a minute earlier, was suddenly subdued. ''Okay.''

''Good girl.'' He sent her a brief smile of approval and headed for his study.

Rooted in place, Eve swallowed an instinctive cry of protest. She longed to shake him until his teeth rattled but, of course, would do no such thing. She'd only been here a week, after all, and John was her employer. It wasn't her place to tell him how to run his life—or raise his daughter.

Yet as she turned toward Lissy, her heart nearly broke in two at the disappointment she could see on the child's face as Lissy watched her father walk away.

''Thanks, Marty. I'll give you a call later in the week after I get the transport arranged. It's been a pleasure doing business with you, too. Be sure and tell Maxine hello.''

Pleasantries complete, John hung up the phone. Feeling the tension in his shoulders, he stretched, then leaned back in his oversize leather desk chair and took yet another look at the columns of figures on his computer screen.

He'd been trying to get Martin Hersher to sell some of his prime breeding stock for more than six months. Now, not only had the Oklahoma rancher finally agreed to part with more than a thousand head, but he'd agreed to do it for an extremely reasonable price.

And how did he feel? Was he pleased? Satisfied? Filled with a sense of triumph?

No. He felt empty, as if he'd just achieved the world's most hollow victory.

He shoved back his chair and climbed to his feet. The thick, hand-knotted Persian rug muffled the sound of his boots as he prowled restlessly around the room, finally coming to a stop at one of the tall, arched windows. Bracing his hands against the frame, he looked out.

With the suddenness so typical of fall, night had fallen in the hour that he and Hersher had spent hammering out a deal. The evening sky stretched overhead like a vast swath of dark velvet, studded with the first faint glimmering stars and a silver slice of moon.

Yet it was the land, vast and ruggedly beautiful in the moonlight, that drew his eye. How many nights had he lain in his narrow bed at the orphanage and promised himself that no matter what it took, someday he was going to amount to something?

Now, thanks to hard work and a talent for playing the stock market, he had all the things he'd once only dreamed about—his own ranch, financial security, a respected position in the community.

And none of it seemed to matter when measured against the happiness of one little kid.

His heart squeezed as he thought about the look that had come over Lissy's face when he'd blown off her offer to look at her new clothes. He knew damn well that a good father never would have done such a thing. A good father would have jumped at the invitation.

He would have told his caller, no matter how important, that he'd have to call back.

He would have put his daughter first.

But not him. Not John MacLaren, hotshot cattle rancher and businessman. As usual, he not only hadn't known the right things to say to her, but when presented with an opportunity for the two of them to spend some time together, he'd leaped at the first opportunity to pass.

And though he knew it was for her own good—that if he had gone to look at her clothes he'd either have said the wrong thing or not known what to say at all, letting her down even more—it didn't make her disappointment any easier to bear. About the best that could be said of the whole sorry performance was that it appeared he'd done one thing right. He'd hired Eve, who, if the cozy little scene he'd walked in on was any indication, seemed to have achieved over the past week the kind of bond with Lissy that he could only imagine.

So what if her unexpected rapport with his daughter also made him feel the way he had as a kid, like an outsider looking in?

He'd survive. He always had.

That is, if he didn't first expire from unrelieved lust.

A self-mocking smile twisted his lips. By the time he'd reached Missoula Friday night, he'd managed to convince himself that his recent reaction to Eve was nothing more than his body's response to being celibate for much too long. What's more, he'd decided a little grimly that it was past time he do something about it—a resolve that had lasted right up until last night, when he'd been approached at the hotel bar by an attractive brunette who'd made her intentions clear with flattering directness.

It had been an unpleasant shock to discover he didn't feel a shred of interest.

Frustrated, he'd gruffly tendered his regrets to the lady, pleading exhaustion while telling himself that he simply liked to be the one in pursuit. He'd almost believed it, too—until he'd walked into his own house, taken one look at Eve and felt the desire he'd just spent forty-eight hours telling himself wasn't reserved solely for her come roaring back to life.

"John?"

Eve's soft voice invaded his thoughts. For a second he thought he'd imagined it. And then she said his name again and he realized he hadn't. More than a little aggravated—she was the last person he wanted to see right now—he stayed where he was. "What?"

"Dinner's ready."

He'd never felt less like eating in his life. "Thanks, but I'll pass. I stopped in Drover on the way home and had a late lunch."

There was a lengthy silence. Yet with a sixth sense he didn't question, he knew she hadn't left.

Reluctantly, he turned. Sure enough, she stood just inside the doorway. And though he knew it was ridiculous, for a split second he could have sworn he saw a flash of longing, a glint of hunger in her eyes. In the next instant it was gone, leaving him feeling even more foolish and frustrated. "Was there something else?"

At his harsh tone, she drew herself up. "As a matter of fact, yes. I was going to talk to you at dinner, but— may I come in?"

He didn't want her here. Not now, when he already

felt dangerously on edge. Yet damned if he had any intention of letting *her* see such weakness. "Suit yourself."

She shut the door and approached. His mood deteriorated even more at the realization that the mere sight of her—the lithe way she walked, the way her pale hair gleamed in the lamplight—turned him on.

Stopping when only a few feet separated them, she glanced up at him. "I thought you might want to look over the receipts for Lissy's new clothes. That way—" her manner was as cool as her clear gray eyes "—you'll at least have some idea what we purchased."

There was no mistaking the censure in her voice. And though he knew he deserved it, coming from her it rankled. "Thanks. You can leave them on my desk on your way out."

"All right." She didn't move.

"Anything else?"

"Yes. I have a favor to ask." Despite the words, she didn't sound in the least like a supplicant.

"And what's that?"

"While I was at home, I got into the habit of riding a few hours a week. If you can spare a horse, I'd like to start again. I—I could use the exercise."

His jaw bunched at the irony of it. Here he was, feeling as if his life was spinning out of control, and she was worried about going horseback riding. "No problem, princess. I'll let them know down at the barn to expect you." He paused, unable to keep the sarcasm out of his voice as he added, "You'll have to be your own groom, though. I don't pay my wranglers to wait on anybody. Particularly not another employee."

Her chin ratcheted up another notch. "I think I can manage."

The hell of it was, he had no doubt she could. As galling as it was to admit, the way she'd handled things this past week had forced him to acknowledge that she wasn't nearly as spoiled or selfish as he wanted to believe.

Not that he'd changed his overall opinion of her. At least where he was concerned, she was still the original ice princess, as evidenced by the way she currently seemed to be looking down at him—no mean feat, given that he towered over her by at least eight inches.

It was just his bad luck that the very air of superiority that set his teeth on edge also made the more primitive part of him want to tame her—atop the nearest horizontal surface.

"Are you done?" he inquired brusquely.

She hesitated, then nodded.

"Good." He stepped around her, strode to his desk, sat down and began to go through a stack of papers. "If you don't mind, I've got work to do."

He felt her eyes on his back. Yet she didn't say another word, simply walked over, set down what he belatedly realized were Lissy's clothing receipts, and exited the room.

Telling himself he was glad she was gone, he took a deep breath to settle himself—only to discover too late that the air was laced with the faint scent of her perfume.

His body hardened, and in that instant he came to a decision.

From now until however long it took for his libido to come to its senses, he'd give Ms. Chandler some serious distance.

Five

"I think that went really well," Eve said to Lissy as they walked out of the barn and began the trek to the house.

"You do?" Lissy's voice was doubtful.

"Uh-huh." The breeze tugged at her hair, and she smiled, enjoying the play of crisp air against her face. Although the afternoon was sunny and mild, the snow line on the surrounding mountains was noticeably lower than it had been a week ago, a reminder that winter was on the way.

"Even though I start to fall off every time Clue trots?" Clue was the small pinto mare that Jeb, the old wrangler who oversaw John's horses, had selected for the child.

"Yes." Eve reached over and squeezed the little girl's shoulder. "You're still learning, sweetie. You just need to relax a little, give it some time—and stop being so hard on yourself. Don't forget, just two weeks ago you were afraid to even touch a horse. Now, after only a handful of lessons, you know how to saddle and bridle one, how to get on and off, how to walk and trot and make the horse go where you want. I'd say that's a lot.''

Almost reluctantly, Lissy nodded. "I s'pose." Despite her agreement, she continued to look pensive.

Eve regarded her with a thoughtful look of her own. There had been a lot going on lately, and suddenly she wondered if perhaps it had been too much. In addition to the sessions with Clue and having Eve help out in her classroom, Lissy had had her new friend Jenny over to play twice in the past ten days. Eve supposed the child had every right to be feeling a little overwhelmed.

"Eve?"

"Hmm?"

"Do you think my dad's mad at me?"

The question was so far from Eve's thoughts that it stopped her dead in her tracks. She swiveled to look at Lissy, dismayed when the child looked back at her and she saw the worry in those big blue eyes. "Oh, sweetie, of course not. Why would you think that?"

"Because." Hunching her shoulders, the little girl stared down at the road, refusing to meet her gaze. "He never did ask to see my new clothes. And even though he said it was okay, he wasn't there for dinner either time that Jenny was. He hasn't even been around enough—" there was a sudden hitch in her voice "—to say good-night to me."

For a moment, Eve didn't know what to say. Then she leaned over and clasped the child's hand, tugging her around so that they were facing each other. "Lissy, listen to me. I am one hundred percent certain your dad is not mad at you.''

''You are?''

''Yes, I am.''

The child swallowed. ''Then do you think…do you think that maybe he just doesn't like me?''

Eve wasn't sure whether to laugh or cry. ''Oh, sweetie, no. *No.* Your dad *loves* you.''

The child considered a moment. ''Then how come he never wants to be with me?''

Eve hesitated. More than anything, she wanted to reassure Lissy. At the same time, instinct told her that if she wanted to retain the girl's trust, she had to tell the truth. ''I know it may seem that way,'' she said slowly. ''But you have to remember, he has this whole big ranch to run. But he does care. That's why he hired me. So I could be here with you when he couldn't.''

''Oh.'' Some— but not all—of the misery on that young face lifted. ''But how come, even when he is around the way he was before you came, he hardly ever talks to me?''

''Well…sometimes it's hard for grown-ups to know what to say to kids.''

''It's not hard for you.''

She smiled. ''True. But then, you and I are both girls. Maybe what I should've said was that sometimes it's hard for grown-up men to know what to say to kids, particularly little girls.''

''Was it hard for your grandpa to talk to you?''

Again, Eve hesitated. ''Well, no, not really,'' she reluctantly admitted. She'd already told Lissy how she'd come at age eight to live with Max after losing her parents in a car accident. ''But my grandpa was a different kind of person than your dad.''

Lissy looked at her questioningly.

Eve tried to decide how best to explain Max's effusive, take-charge personality in a way that the child could understand. "With my grandpa, the problem was never getting him to talk...it was getting him to listen. He'd sweep into a room, give you a great big bear hug, and then he'd start telling you what he had planned for you."

"That sounds nice."

"Sometimes. But my grandfather could also be very stubborn. So there were times—" more times than Eve wanted to remember "—when you found yourself doing what he wanted you to, rather than what *you* thought was best for you." A faint frown marred her brow as she heard the truth in her own words.

Lissy, however, wasn't concerned with such distinctions. She gave a wistful little sigh. "I just wish my dad would give me a hug, even once. And that he'd talk to me. Even just a little."

There was such longing in the little girl's voice that Eve found herself reminded of the previous Sunday and Lissy's expression when John had chosen business over her. And suddenly she knew that she'd been wrong when she'd told herself that it wasn't her place to intercede with John on Lissy's behalf.

Wrong—and spineless.

Because she'd made a vow the day she buried her grandfather. She'd promised herself from then on, if she ever again cared about someone, she was going to pay attention to that person's hopes and needs.

She knew it didn't sound like much. At least, not until one took into account that for the past few years the only person she'd looked out for was herself. Thanks to her trust fund, she'd spent her time gliding through life like a leaf on a wind current. She'd skied in Switzerland, sailed the turquoise waters of the Aegean, observed endangered gorillas in Uganda and attended fashion shows in Paris. While it hadn't been a life-style that encouraged close relationships, she'd done what she wanted when she wanted, and she'd enjoyed every minute.

Everything had seemed perfect until she'd gotten the phone call informing her that Max had died from a massive heart attack. Grief-stricken, she'd rushed home—and crashed headlong into a massive wall of reality. While she'd been off enjoying herself, the man who'd always been her rock had been losing everything he'd worked seventy years to achieve. What's more, he'd deliberately hidden the truth from her, obviously believing she couldn't handle it.

Eve had been shocked, angry, heartsick. Yet as the weeks had passed and she'd had to grapple with the overwhelming financial mess that was her inheritance, she'd gradually come to accept what she couldn't change. And to acknowledge that even though she'd been doing what she'd thought her grandfather wanted, she'd let him down by not being stronger— and by living her life as if it were one endless summer vacation. It hadn't been much of a leap to see that it was time to stop playing and start acting like a grown-up.

That realization had led to her vow, which seemed especially meaningful now.

Because she cared about Lissy—more than she'd cared about anyone for a very long time. And, if she were honest with herself, she had to admit that she'd been selfish the past pair of weeks. Rather than worrying about the effect of John's absences on Lissy, she'd been secretly relieved he was making himself scarce because it meant she didn't have to deal with his effect on *her.*

Except this wasn't about her. And it was time she remembered that and got her priorities straight.

She looked over at Lissy. "I honestly don't know if your dad's ever going to be the kind of dad who gives lots of hugs," she said gently. "But I am sure, now that the weekend is here and he doesn't have to be somewhere the way he did last weekend, he'll set some time aside just for you."

As easy to read as a picture book, Lissy's face reflected a combination of skepticism and hope. "You are?"

"I am," Eve said firmly. She intended to make sure it happened.

No matter what she had to do.

John shrugged out of his coat and tossed it onto a hook in the mudroom.

A wedge of light poured through the door from the kitchen, cutting a path through the room's darkness. The house was quiet, for which he was profoundly grateful. Today, like every other day since he'd returned from Missoula, he'd worked a full eighteen hours, and he could feel it in every aching muscle. Still, it was worth it. He'd put some serious space between himself and Eve, just the way he'd intended.

He'd also managed to get quite a lot accomplished. Although his hired hands had grumbled that he was pushing too hard, almost every mile of fence that surrounded the ranch's perimeter had now been checked and mended as needed. The various feed stations were fully stocked, and the watering holes cleared of any debris and obstructions. Come Monday morning, they'd start moving the herd down from the summer pastures.

And after that? Well, in addition to normal daily chores, there was wood to be chopped for both this place and the bunkhouse, half a dozen vehicles to be winterized, gas generators and kerosene heaters to be cleaned and filled, food and emergency supplies to be purchased.

He expelled a tired breath. Hell, all he had to do was give it another month or two, and he might be worn out enough that the mere thought of Eve would finally stop making him ache.

With an exasperated shake of his head, he pulled his feet out of his boots, grabbed a pair of clean jeans out of the laundry basket and walked into the bathroom. Scant minutes later he stepped naked into the tiled shower enclosure, groaning with pleasure as the hot water poured over his back and shoulders. He let his head fall forward and gave himself over to the luxurious sensation.

It was a long time before he found the strength to reach for the bar of soap on the shelf in the corner.

Not until the water began to cool did he reluctantly turn the spigot off and climb out. Yawning, he did a haphazard job drying off and yanked on his jeans, not bothering to fasten more than the first three buttons. Scrubbing at his damp hair with a towel, he opened the door and ambled out. He walked several paces, the granite floor cool against his bare feet, before the realization that he wasn't alone brought him up short.

"I thought I heard you come in," Eve said softly.

She stood in the kitchen doorway. Her pale hair was loose, tumbling like a silken cape to her shoulders, and she was wearing a pair of leggings and a loose-knit sweater the same soft gray as her eyes. Backlit as she was, the enticing shape of her body was perfectly outlined.

He lowered the towel. "What are you doing up?"

"It's Friday."

"So?"

"So it's only 9:30. There's no school tomorrow, and I told Lissy she could stay up a little later on the off chance that you'd be home in time to say goodnight."

Annoyance over her bossiness couldn't compete with the guilt he carried about Lissy. While he didn't doubt that making himself scarce had been the right thing to do, there was also no denying that he'd missed not seeing more of his daughter. He'd looked in on her every night before he turned in, and again in the morning before he'd lit out for the day, but even he knew that watching her sleep wasn't the same as actually being with her. "Sure. I'd like that."

Approval—and something that looked oddly like relief—flashed across her face. "Good."

He waited for her to leave. She didn't.

Instead, her gaze remained fixed on his face. And though there was nothing even remotely provocative about her manner, her mere presence, along with the dim light, her husky voice and the unintentional display of her body, had desire slamming through him.

He came to a sudden decision. "As a matter of fact, I'll do it right now." Straightening decisively, he tossed the towel onto the washer and headed for the door, intent on reaching the lighted oasis of the kitchen before he did something irreparably stupid.

"But I also wanted to—John, wait!" she exclaimed as he brushed past her.

Out of the corner of his eye, he saw her reach for him. And just for an instant he was tempted to stop, to experience her touch, to find out if his reaction would be as intense as he suspected.

Except that he was very much afraid that one touch wouldn't be enough. Just as he was very aware that his control was marginal; already he could feel his body respond—and he was only *thinking* about having her hands on him, damn it.

He jerked sideways, out of her reach, careful to put a few feet between them before he finally turned to face her. "What? What do you want, Eve?" Self-imposed restraint made his voice harsh.

There was no way for Eve to know that, of course. Predictably, the lush line of her mouth thinned out in the face of his impatience. "I was just hoping that if you had a moment, we could talk."

"No." He was shaking his head before she finished the sentence. "Not tonight," he amended. "I'm beat."

She frowned. "Tomorrow then?"

"Sure." He walked away even as he said it, passing into the kitchen and quickly crossing the great room. He didn't slow until he reached the hall leading to the bedrooms.

Lissy's door was the first one on the right, well before his own. Taking a grip on his emotions, he thrust every thought of Eve out of his head, assumed a neutral expression and looked in.

Not only was the little girl still awake, but she'd clearly been watching for him. Although the room was heavily shadowed, illuminated only by a small lamp on her bedside table, there was no missing the uncertain little smile that flitted across her face. "You came."

Nodding, he stepped across the threshold.

"I was hoping you would," she murmured, burrowing deeper into the covers as he gingerly approached the bed. "Even though Eve said I shouldn't count on it 'cause you were real, real busy taking care of the ranch and everything."

He felt a pinch of surprise. Surprise that she'd missed him. And that Eve of all people would bother to make an excuse for him.

He reached down and awkwardly smoothed the blanket over one small shoulder. "It's late," he said gruffly. "You better get to sleep."

"Okay." Despite her ready agreement, she didn't close her eyes. Instead, she looked up at him with an air of expectancy, as if she were waiting for something.

Helplessly, he looked back. "What?" he said finally.

She ducked her head, looking very young and uncertain. "You—you can give me a kiss good-night, if you want to. Eve always does."

Squashing the image of Eve pursing her soft pink lips for a kiss, he cleared his throat. "Yeah. Sure." Exceedingly aware of how small and delicate Lissy was, and how small and delicate he wasn't, and suddenly self-conscious about his lack of a shirt, he carefully braced an arm on either side of her, leaned over and gently touched his lips to her brow.

She smelled of toothpaste, talcum powder and innocence. He squeezed his eyes shut, wishing yet again that things were different, that *he* was different, that he could be the kind of father who could actually gather her close and tell her how very special she was, instead of just thinking about it.

But she was only seven years old; such fierce emotion coming from him would probably scare her to death. And he'd cut off his right arm rather than scare her even a little bit.

Reining himself in, he straightened. "Good night, Lis."

There was a heartbeat of silence. Then she gave a little sigh that was so filled with disappointment even he couldn't miss it. "Night," she whispered. Rolling onto her side, she pulled the covers to her chin and closed her eyes.

John stood, rooted in place by the ache in his heart as he stared down at the still form of his daughter. Although he wasn't sure how, he'd clearly just let her down. For a second the pain was so great, he was unable to breathe.

Then, through an act of will, he shook it off and forced himself to move, bitterly aware that it wouldn't matter if he stood here forever— he still wouldn't have a clue what he'd just done wrong.

He reached for the lamp switch, only to freeze at a faint sound from the hallway. He swung around to find Eve standing in the hallway, staring straight at him. For a second their gazes locked, and then she hurried away.

Yet he knew from the look on her face that she'd been a witness to his failure.

With angry despair, he switched off the light and headed for his room.

Eve slid the last clean plate out of the dishwasher and added it to the pair in her free hand. Taking a secure grip on the trio, she carried them to the cabinet and put them away.

Outside, a heavy cloud curtain darkened the morning sky. Inside, the room was cloaked in shadows, giving it a somber feeling that perfectly suited her mood.

She returned to the dishwasher. Pulling the silverware holder free, she set it on the counter and began putting the various utensils away.

Although she was getting a late start on her morning chores, she'd been awake for hours, after a long night spent tossing and turning. And no matter how hard she tried to convince herself that she'd slept poorly due to frustration over her failure to speak to John about Lissy, she knew better.

The plain truth was, she couldn't quit thinking about the look she'd seen on John's face last night when she'd looked in and seen him gazing down at Lissy. In the brief time that she'd observed him, she'd seen tenderness, confusion, regret—and stark, unadulterated longing. It had opened her mind to the possibility that there was a whole other side of him.

And she didn't want that to be the case. Because, try as she might to pretend otherwise, even before last night her attraction to him had stubbornly been refusing to go away.

And she was darned if she understood it. So far he'd been brusque, aloof and shown her all the warmth of an ice cube. She didn't care for the way he treated his daughter. Heck, as far as that went, she didn't like the way he treated *her,* always assuming the worst about her character.

And yet, after three weeks under his roof, the magnetism he held for her hadn't diminished. Worse, there were some things about him she actually admired. He worked harder than anyone she'd ever known. He was generous to a fault, paying excellent wages and doing whatever it took to make certain working conditions on the Bar M were top rate. What's more, a chance remark by Mitch Mason, his foreman, had revealed that many of the ranch's hired hands came from the Lander Boys' Home, hinting at a depth of loyalty she never would have suspected.

Oh, and don't forget his other sterling quality, she thought dryly. *He can make your nipples stand up and pay attention just by walking into a room.*

She sighed, finally facing the crux of her problem.

She was twenty-five years old. And while she wasn't a virgin, so far in her experience she'd found sex to be highly overrated. Oh, she was willing to concede that under the right circumstances it might be pleasurable enough—if your tastes ran to being sweaty, undignified and having your privacy invaded.

So far, hers hadn't.

Of course, John was nothing at all like the men who'd pursued her in the past. Those men had been polished and sophisticated, with salon-cut hair and manicured nails. They'd approached sex like some sort of parlor game, as if it were nothing more than an entertaining way to fritter the time away. They'd been far too polite to press for a response she wouldn't, or couldn't, give.

John wasn't polite about anything. He was hard, tough, real, and every instinct she possessed insisted that making love with him wouldn't have a thing to do with either courtesy or restraint.

Not that she planned on testing her theory anytime soon, she told herself hastily. Or anytime at all, for that matter. Although she might be tempted if doing it meant she could stop thinking about it.

The sound of the back door slamming shut made her jump. Hastily putting the last pair of coffee cups away, she struggled to regain her composure as she heard the cupboards being banged open and shut in the mudroom. Seconds later John strode into the kitchen.

To her relief, he was so intent on his own thoughts he gave her only a cursory nod before he tossed his work gloves onto the counter, walked over to the open pantry door, hit the light switch and disappeared inside.

By the time he reappeared, she had herself and her intemperate thoughts well under control. "Good morning," she said with a polite smile.

He brushed past her and yanked open a door to one of the overhead kitchen cabinets. "Morning."

She turned to keep him in view. "What are you doing?"

"Looking for a Band-Aid. I thought there was a box of them in the mudroom. But I'm damned if I can find it."

"Oh." Skirting around him, she retrieved the box in question off the counter and handed it to him. "Sorry. I took them after I nicked my finger on a paring knife last night. I should have put them back."

"Don't worry about it." Taking the box, he pried open the top and dumped the contents on the counter.

It was then that she noticed the blood oozing angrily from an ugly gash in the back of his right hand. Ridiculously, she felt an immediate surge of concern. "What happened?"

He selected the largest of the adhesive strips and

shrugged, dismissing her worry. "I caught it on a nail. The damn thing keeps bleeding on everything." He removed the backing and awkwardly tried to position the rectangular bandage over the wound with his left hand.

Eve hesitated. The last thing she wanted to do was touch him. At the same time, they were both adults, he was hurt—and she'd rather parade naked down Lander's main street than behave in a way that made him suspect how unsettled he made her feel. "Here. Let me." She reached over and plucked the bandage away before she could lose her nerve.

His head came up and he glowered at her. "I can do it myself."

So much for that softer side. The man was as tough as nails. "I'm sure you can," she said evenly, determined not to lose her composure. "But don't you think you ought to disinfect it first?" Not waiting for an answer, she went and got the first-aid kit out of the cupboard.

Lips pursed, he didn't say a word as she opened it, motioned him over to the sink, cradled his hand in hers and poured a liberal amount of hydrogen peroxide over the cut.

As the seconds passed and she waited for the disinfectant to work, she discovered her resolve had its limits, however. She grew increasingly aware of his proximity, of the warmth radiating from his skin, of the size and strength of his hand. And she found herself wondering what those long, calloused fingers would feel like against her breast—

She released him as if scalded and said the first thing she could to fill the silence. "You were up early this morning."

He made a sound that could have been a yes.

Gesturing for him to step back over to where the Band-Aid pile was spread out on the counter, she gingerly patted the back of his hand dry with a paper towel and reached for the antibacterial ointment. "I'm sorry you cut yourself. Still, I'm glad you're here. We really do need to talk."

"About what?"

She tore open a bandage and carefully covered the deepest part of the wound before she answered. "Lissy."

She felt his arm tense beneath her fingertips a second before he pulled his hand away and took a step back. "What about her?"

"Well, you've hardly spent any time at all with her the past few weeks."

He stiffened. "I've been busy."

His stance, his expression, his tone—all warned her to back off. And though the voice of reason told her that it was the height of foolishness to press him, she couldn't seem to let it go. "When won't you be busy?"

"I don't know. Later."

"When later?"

"I don't know." Although his voice was even when he spoke, his blue eyes glittered with warning. "Maybe tonight. Maybe tomorrow. Maybe not until next week."

"Tomorrow's my day off."

"Yeah, well, I've been meaning to talk to you about that. There's this bull I need to take a look at over in Lager—"

"No."

One black eyebrow shot up. "What?"

"I have plans."

"So cancel them."

She stared at him in disbelief. Half a dozen pointed replies sprang to mind, but before she could settle on one that wasn't guaranteed to get her fired, a movement across the room caught her eye. She looked over and saw Lissy padding toward them. A quick glance at John showed that he, too, had caught sight of his daughter.

Her face still blurred with sleep, the child climbed up on one of the padded bar stools on the far side of the counter. She glanced from one to the other, looking endearingly sweet with her hair standing up in every direction. "What's the matter?"

John spoke without hesitation. "Nothing." The finality in his voice—and the warning glance he threw Eve's way—made it clear that as far as he was concerned, the discussion was over.

His autocratic manner set Eve's teeth on edge, and all of a sudden the thought of him having the last word—yet again—was intolerable. "Actually, we were just talking about tomorrow. It's my day off, but your father has some business he needs to take care of." Just for a second, she wondered about the wisdom of what she was about to do, then shrugged it off. She'd tried to appeal to John's reason; it wasn't her fault that he didn't have any. "That's why I'm going to take a few hours off today."

She felt John's gaze snap to her face. "What?" he demanded, in nearly the same breath that Lissy said, "You are?"

"Yes, I am," she said to the child. She turned to the child's father. "I haven't had a day off since I started," she pointed out in a level voice. "And there are some things I need to take care of."

He was silent. She crossed her fingers, praying he was going to be reasonable, only to have her hopes dashed when he said caustically, "What's the big emergency, princess? Chip your nail polish?"

Inexplicably, the words hurt—and that made her angry. She lifted her chin. "As a matter of fact, yes. How charming of you to notice."

To her satisfaction, his mouth clamped shut.

"But...when are you going?" Lissy again glanced between them. Her worried expression made it clear she sensed the tension that stretched between them like an invisible wire.

"Now." Suiting action to words, Eve picked up her purse off the counter.

"But I'm s'posed to go to Jenny's this afternoon to play and have dinner, remember?"

"Don't worry. I'll be back by three. That'll be plenty of time to take you."

"Oh."

"In the meantime, you and your dad can spend some time together."

"Oh." Again, Lissy glanced between them. Only this time, the gaze she sent John's way held burgeoning anticipation. "Okay."

It was enough to give Eve the courage she needed to leave.

Six

True to her word, Eve was back in plenty of time to take Lissy to Jenny's.

Staunchly ignoring the butterflies in her stomach, she parked the ancient Wagoneer next to John's shiny pickup and told herself—for what had to be the hundredth time in the past six hours—that she'd done the right thing.

Not that she was particularly proud of the way she'd backed John into a corner. Common sense—as well as a very clear memory of the look in his eyes when she'd announced she was leaving—suggested she would be wise to pursue a more diplomatic course in the future. Still, it wasn't as if he'd left her any other options. If he had, she wouldn't have felt pressed to take such drastic action.

With that thought in mind, she picked up her purse, climbed from the Jeep and walked resolutely into the house, letting the screen door slap shut behind her to announce her presence. Yet by the time she reached the great room, it was clear the place was deserted. She was puzzled for all of a second, until she realized that John wasn't the type to hang around inside under any circumstances—and certainly not to wait for her. Obviously, he and Lissy were out on the property somewhere. Although she knew it didn't speak well of her character, as she headed for her bedroom she felt a little surge of satisfaction at the thought of them together.

She hadn't walked more than a few feet down the hallway, however, when some primitive instinct warned her there was someone else in the house after all. Instinctively, she glanced over her shoulder, but there was no one there. She turned back around, shaking her head at her foolishness—only to jerk to a halt as John stepped out of his bedroom at the end of the corridor.

He, too, stopped short when he saw her. "You're back."

Her stomach plummeted at his cool, clipped tone. It didn't take a genius to realize he was still angry. "Yes." She took a calming breath, determined to remain composed no matter what. "I said I'd be home by now."

He didn't say a word, simply watched her.

"How did it go with you and Lissy?"

"We managed."

He didn't seem inclined to say anything more, and because she knew the child would fill in the details, she let it go. "That's good."

He crossed his arms. "You get your business taken care of?"

"Yes. I did."

Again, he was silent. Eve wondered if he was purposefully trying to intimidate her or if it was just a natural talent. She tried to inject some lightness into her voice. "So, is Lissy ready to go?" She took a step toward the child's closed door, only to freeze as John abruptly cut the distance between them in half.

"Not so fast." Although several feet still separated them, he suddenly seemed far too close. "There are a few things we need to get straight."

She lifted her chin, not liking his tone. And liking even less that she was far too aware of everything about him, from the way a gleaming lick of inky hair angled over his forehead to the manner in which the clearly delineated muscles in his arms and shoulders flexed beneath his black T-shirt as he leaned toward her. "Like what?"

"Let's start with the fact that *you* work for me. And what I say goes. If I tell you I'm busy, or I have something I need to do, that's it. *You* don't decide my priorities."

Eve opened her mouth to protest, then shut it again. While she hardly agreed with his take on things, she knew she'd pushed things earlier. Given that she'd accomplished what she set out to, and she still had her job, she could afford to be magnanimous. "Fair enough."

Incredibly, his eyes narrowed. "Don't patronize me, Eve. And just so there's no misunderstanding, don't you ever again try to use Lissy, or her presence, to manipulate me the way you did this morning. Because I swear, if you do—" he took another step toward her as if to underscore his point "—I'll fire you."

Well, that was clear enough. So was the realization

that she didn't like being threatened. But again, under the circumstances, she was willing to let it pass. "Fine."

There was another long silence as they considered each other.

"Is that it?" she said finally.

He nodded.

"I'd better get Lissy then. It's time for us to go."

"That won't be necessary." Once more his voice stopped her, this time as she reached for the doorknob. "She's not here."

"What?" She turned to look at him.

"She's already at Jenny's. I ran her over."

"When?"

His eyes hooded over, and she had a sudden premonition that she wasn't going to like the answer. "This morning. After breakfast."

"What?" Usually she was slow to anger, but now she felt her temper ignite. And as angry as she was at him, she was even angrier with herself as it dawned on her that while she'd thought she was so clever by forcing father and daughter together, the truth was she'd unthinkingly set Lissy up for another rejection. "Why?"

He drew himself up. "She'll have a hell of a lot better time there than she would here, hanging around with me."

"John! You're her father—"

"So? It's not like we have tons to talk about. She's not exactly interested in the price of hay, and I don't know jack about Barbie."

"But it doesn't matter! Not to Lissy. She just wants to spend time with you. Surely you must know that.

It's written all over her face every time she looks at you!''

"I don't want to discuss it," he said flatly.

She stared at him in amazement. "Well that's too bad, because I do, and as you were so kind to point out, I'm your employee—not your slave. What's more, I care about your daughter, and she happens to care about you, which you'd know if you'd just taken the time to talk to me the way I asked twice in the past twenty-four hours!"

"I was tired last night."

"I understand that. But you said we'd talk today—"

"Well excuse the hell out of me for not making you my first priority!" For the first time the icy control he had on his emotions slipped a little bit.

She threw up her hands. "Oh, for—! I want you to make Lissy your first priority! Good heavens, you're all each other has. She's starving for your attention, not to mention your affection—"

"Damn it, Eve! I don't need you to tell me I'm never going to be father of the year. But what I did was for Lissy's own good, and that's all I intend to say about it!" His face set, his mouth a straight line, he made to walk past her.

"No, John, wait!" Eve didn't stop to think; she simply reacted. "If you'd just listen to me, if you'd just take the time to really think about your daughter—" She stepped sideways into his path.

Unable to stop his momentum, he twisted sideways to keep from running her down, and wound up bumping her hip with his thigh. Thrown off balance, she reached out to save herself.

John wasn't prepared as her smooth, soft hand closed around the bare skin of his upper arm. Already dangerously on edge, he felt an explosion of warmth spill through him.

"Don't," he said hoarsely as all of his senses responded to her touch. He swung around to ward her off, but the action only served to send her cool, slender fingers skimming down his arm.

And then they were face-to-face, so close he could feel the warm whisper of her breath through the thin cotton molding his chest.

She made a faint little sound. He looked down, frozen in place as her gaze drifted over his torso and her lips promptly parted. A faint flush of color rose in her cheeks. To his shock, her nipples pebbled.

He ordered himself to move. To get away. Now, before he did something rash.

Then she looked up. He could see the agitation, the anger, the uncertainty in her eyes. But he could also see her awareness of him as a man. And—the sight made his throat go tight—something that could best be described as speculation, as if she were wondering what they'd be like together...

It was too damn much. All the emotions he'd been struggling to contain seemed to fuse into one overpowering need. He didn't want to think. He wanted to taste her. Just once.

He locked his arm around her waist and yanked her close, only to freeze as her hand came up to splay across his chest.

"No." Her voice was barely more than a whisper, but the pewter gaze she raised to his held a spark of determination. "Not unless you can accept that I'm not giving up on you and Lissy. That this conversation...isn't over. Just on hold."

His eyes narrowed, but she didn't flinch, and he felt

an unwanted kernel of respect for her. Slowly, he nodded, a jolt going through him as her voice became even huskier as she murmured, "Good."

Her hand rose, cupped his cheek, and the next thing he knew his mouth had found hers and he was lost to everything else as he claimed what he'd only fantasized about for so long.

Her lips were smooth and pliant, every bit as soft as he'd always imagined. For untold seconds he savored the sweetness of her taste, the breathy little moan she couldn't contain as his teeth claimed her full lower lip, the provocative way her mouth clung to his as he relentlessly deepened the kiss.

Then it was his turn to shudder as her arms came up and locked around his neck. One slender hand gripped the hair at the base of his skull, urging him closer as she molded her body to his.

The shock of it was almost more than he could bear. His mouth opened over hers and his tongue stabbed inside, instigating an evocative rhythm. He felt the erect tips of her breasts press into his chest and her foot start to climb the back of his thigh.

Heat scorched the last rational thought from his mind.

Wedging his hand between them, he slid it under her shirt. Her skin was warm, smooth, taut, like sunwarmed satin. Consumed with the need to touch her, he forgot to breathe as he cupped the ripe weight of one breast in his palm and rubbed his fingertips against the pebbled velvet of her nipple.

She whimpered and crowded even closer.

He couldn't hold back any longer. Releasing her breast, he reached down with both hands, gripped her high, round little fanny in his hands and lifted her up, rubbing her against the iron-hard ridge barely contained by the worn denim of his jeans.

The heated contact jolted through him, an overload of sensation so intense, he was almost able to ignore her breathless "oh" and the way she stiffened slightly in his arms.

Almost, but not quite. He wanted her, yes. But more than that, he wanted her willing; his pride dug in its heels at the thought of anything less. He tore his mouth away from hers. "What's wrong?"

Denied his lips, she slicked a kiss down the line of his jaw. "Nothing," she said breathlessly.

"Do you want me to stop?"

"No."

"Are you sure?"

"*Yes.*" Her mouth slid to his throat and settled over the pulse thundering there.

For half a second, he was riveted in place. And then his whole body caught fire. He picked her up, carried her into his bedroom, shouldered the door shut and set her down. Without a word, he began to strip off his clothes.

Eve drew a shaky breath and pressed a finger to her tingling lips. In some dim recess of her mind she realized this was going to complicate everything. And yet right now she couldn't bring herself to care. For eight years she'd wondered about him, about this. It had been John who, without so much as a touch, had awakened her burgeoning sexuality and fueled her every adolescent fantasy. It had been his image against which she'd measured every other man in the years since. Measured—and always found lacking...

She watched, unable to move, unable to breathe, as he stripped his T-shirt over his head. She was peripherally aware of the room around her, of the series of arched windows looking out toward the mountains, of the simple lines of the oak furniture, of the richly patterned blue-and-black comforter on the big bed.

It was the emerging sight of his bare chest that claimed her attention, however. She'd seen it before, of course. She'd seen the way the sun-bronzed skin stretched taut over his broad shoulders and the hard, sculpted muscles of his arms. She'd seen the carved slab of his pectorals and that flat, washboard abdomen punctuated by the shallow navel and the tantalizing line of fine, jet-black hair.

But this was the first time she'd had license to touch it, the first time she'd had license to touch *him.*

The realization shuddered through her, and then she was moving, closing the distance between them. Busy with the buttons on his jeans, he gave a jerk of surprise as she slid her fingers over the satin flesh of his sides, trapping his hands between the two of them. And then she was flush up against him. She gave into temptation and pressed her face into the smooth curve of his chest.

It felt like the most natural thing in the world to rub her cheek against all that hot, velvety skin, to part her lips and forge a chain of kisses along his collarbone, to run her palms up the steely curves of his arms. She vaguely registered his hands at her waist, tugging open her slacks, pushing them down, helping her as she toed off her shoes and slid her legs free.

There was nothing vague about her reaction as his hands slid up the back of her bare thighs and over her naked behind, however. Gasping, she buried her face in his throat and raised her arms as he slipped her

T-shirt up and over her head and pulled it and her bra away.

And just like that she was standing before him without a stitch of clothing. She might have felt shy, but she didn't have time as he reached down and tipped up her chin and she saw the look on his face.

His mouth was compressed, his eyes intent, the skin over his nose stretched tight with need while his eyes gleamed like twin slices of blue fire. It was the look of a conqueror, of a man who wouldn't be denied.

He reached around and released the clip holding back her hair. "Damn." With a gentleness totally at odds with that fierce expression, he spread her hair over her shoulders. "I always thought you were beautiful, princess. But I never realized..." Swallowing hard, he reached down, pressed the pad of his thumb to the stiff, aching point of her nipple and rubbed, his gaze never leaving her face.

Pleasure, unexpected and overwhelming, rocketed through her. She swayed toward him. "John. Please."

His control shattered. His arms came around her and the next thing she knew he was lifting her up. His mouth opened over her throat, hot and insistent as it slid hungrily downward over the notch of her collarbone and feasted on the slope of her breast.

She instinctively locked her legs around his waist as his lips latched onto her nipple. She cried out and arched her back. Weaving her fingers into the cool, heavy silk of his hair, she urged him closer as he began to walk toward the bed.

Seconds later he was bearing her down onto the king-size mattress. Only vaguely did she register the cool press of the comforter beneath her back. Her senses were fixed on John: the taste of him on her lips, the raspy sound of his breath, the solid wedge of his stomach between her thighs.

She watched, heart pounding, as he rocked upright and yanked at the fastenings on his jeans. With one violent shove, he shucked them down along with his briefs. A second later he was leaning forward. He slid his hands beneath her hips and she felt the broad tip of his erection bump up against her welcoming wetness.

"Oh." She couldn't contain the soft breathy sound as he pressed forward and she felt the first thick invading slide of him.

His head came up. Their eyes locked and then he was shifting forward, his mouth taking hers at the same time he thrust his hips and seated himself all the way inside her.

The pleasure was intense, immediate and totally outside the realm of her previous experience. She gave a cry of surprise and dug her fingers into the rock-hard curve of his buttocks, only to cry out again as he shifted and slid his hands under her hips, lifting her up to meet him as he began to thrust.

And then she couldn't breathe, she couldn't think, she could only feel. There was the hot brand of John's mouth at her throat, the cool brush of his hair against her jaw, the firm grip of his big calloused hands, the stomach-hollowing advance and retreat of his sex.

Just as she'd always suspected, there was nothing polite or restrained about what they were sharing. With every surge of his powerful body he was laying claim to her in the most elemental way, and everything that was female in her responded. She felt a heightened sense of urgency, a growing need that had her straining toward him, a building ache that made her dig her heels into the mattress and sob his name.

And then pleasure slammed into her. Her senses exploded. Somewhere off in the distance she heard herself scream with satisfaction. Yet before she could fully grasp the meaning of that sound, much less claim it as her own, another wave rolled through her, stronger and more explosive than the first. Locking her arms around John's neck, she arched upward, holding onto him for dear life as sensation after sensation rocked her.

He continued to thrust heavily into her. She felt her body contract around him, and suddenly he stiffened and his whole big body began to shake. He threw back his head, lifting her off the bed as he bit off a hoarse shout of completion.

Moments later he collapsed, holding her tight as he rolled onto his side. Tangled together, her head pillowed on his shoulder, they lay there, their breath coming in noisy gasps.

Minutes passed. Their breathing quieted. As it did, the pleasurable haze clouding Eve's mind slowly began to lift, while the reality of what had just happened began to sink in.

Beside her, she felt John shift. She bit off an automatic protest as he let go of her and rolled away, the mattress dipping beneath his weight.

With a reluctance she didn't want to analyze, she opened her eyes.

He was sitting on the edge of the bed, his broad, bronzed back flexing as he leaned down to yank off his boots and strip away his jeans. Straightening, he sat for a moment as if to compose himself before finally turning to face her.

To her surprise, although his expression was as guarded as ever, she would have sworn that there was a hint of vulnerability in those brilliant blue eyes. Yet before she could be certain, the phone suddenly rang, the bell shrill in the stark silence. With a look of exasperation, John twisted back around and snatched the receiver off the nightstand. "MacLaren."

Eve let out a breath she hadn't realized she was holding, grateful for the unexpected respite. Tuning out his one-sided conversation, she tried to sort out what she was feeling.

Not too surprisingly, her old self, the contained, self-protective, sane one, was urgently insisting they needed to talk about what had just happened, to agree at the very least that this had been a big mistake.

Yet her new self, a wild, elemental creature she barely recognized, refused to listen. *You've waited a long time to be with him,* it whispered. *Why not give it some time and see what happens? After all, you were wrong about him wanting you. Maybe you're wrong about other things, as well. You'll never know if you don't give it a chance....*

She looked over as he hung up the phone. "Everything okay?" she asked quietly.

"Yeah." He turned around. "That was Lis. She's going to spend the night at Jenny's."

She thought about it, but only for a second. "I suppose, under the circumstances, that's probably a good idea."

"Yeah. I guess it is." He cleared his throat. "So...are you all right?"

She nodded. "Uh-huh. What about you?"

"Me?" The question seemed to surprise him. "I'm fine."

"Good."

Silently, they considered each other. And then, as if he couldn't stop himself, his gaze slid over her naked body, leaving a trail of goose bumps in its wake.

There was no mistaking his appreciation for what he was seeing; his sex stirred to bold, flattering life. But even without that, she would have recognized the hunger suddenly burning in his eyes.

Because she felt it, too.

Yet it was also clear, from the suddenly austere set of his mouth, that he didn't intend to give in to it. "Eve—"

In that instant, she made up her mind. Reaching up, she pressed her fingers to his lips. "Don't. There'll be plenty of time to talk later."

He searched her face. "Are you sure?"

"Yes."

For a long moment he still hesitated. And then he turned his head and unexpectedly pressed his lips to the center of her palm. "All right."

She considered that exquisitely gentle caress, so at odds with his steady, dispassionate voice and felt her last little reservation melt away. With a soft sigh, she wrapped her fingers around the back of his neck and urged him closer.

And then he was rolling her beneath him and his mouth was on hers, hot and hungry, and everything else faded away.

* * *

John came awake with a jerk.

Momentarily disoriented, he lay in the darkness with his eyes wide open, waiting for his mind to catch up with the rest of his body. In the next instant it happened, and with sudden clarity he knew he was in his own house, in his own room, between the sheets of his own bed.

And that the silken shape curled against him was Eve's.

A glance at the digital clock on his dresser told him it was going on midnight. He blinked as he realized he'd slept nearly four hours. But then, he'd been worn down to a sliver after that last bout of lovemaking. Unlike their first explosive encounter, they'd gone slow, taking their time, letting the tension build and build as they explored each other. It had been exquisite torture—and the most intimate experience he'd ever had with a woman.

He slowly let out his breath.

For as long as he could remember, except for a short time as a very young boy when he'd foolishly believed his mother would recognize her mistake and come back for him, he'd dealt with life straight on, refusing to back away no matter how harsh the reality.

But this… Damn but it was hard to wrap his mind around. For so many years, Eve's dislike had been a given.

Yet lying here now, with her hand twined in his and her hair draped over his chest, he could suddenly see how it could be like one of the trick pictures his psychology teacher had sprung on him back in high school.

He'd been asked to look at an image; he had and

he'd seen a goblet. He'd been told to look again, and he'd seen the exact same thing. It hadn't been until it had been pointed out to him that he'd seen that his "goblet" could also be the silhouettes of two identical faces looking in opposite directions.

It had been so many years ago that he couldn't remember now exactly what that exercise had been meant to prove. But he suspected it had something to do with getting locked into a single perspective and seeing only what you expected.

Even though the truth might be more complicated. Like a beautiful girl who'd feigned antipathy to mask attraction. And a young man too proud to look beyond the obvious.

Still, it was old news. Instead of focusing on the past, he ought to be deciding what to do next.

The answer should have been easy, given that he never should have allowed this to happen in the first place. Having failed that, he should end things right now, before they became even more complicated. After all, he wasn't in the market for any kind of committed relationship, having long ago judged—accurately as it turned out—that his chances of making someone a good husband would be on a par with him being a good father. And there was no reason someone like Eve—beautiful, intelligent, educated—should settle for anything less.

His mouth twisted at the irony of him suddenly feeling protective of her. But then, tonight he'd found out that she was far more vulnerable and far less experienced than he'd ever imagined. He also now knew that he was the first man ever to give her pleasure. It made him feel all knotted up inside, as purely primitive male satisfaction warred with an unexpected sense of obligation.

A sense of obligation that was very likely misplaced, he reminded himself. Because it wasn't as if Eve had made any declarations of love herself. Hell, they'd barely talked. For all he knew, she might wake up at any moment, announce that she'd come to her senses and inform him that this had been a big mistake.

Which would probably be for the best. So why did he hate the idea?

He was damned if he knew. But then, he supposed he could be excused for feeling a little fuzzy-headed. It had been a long time since he'd been with a woman. And even if it hadn't been, he'd never experienced the sort of pleasure he had with Eve. Hell, he'd been so far gone during that first encounter that he hadn't even given a thought to birth control, which was a first for him—and a matter that ought to be a major cause for concern.

Only he didn't feel concern. Instead, like some sort of caveman, he felt an irrational surge of satisfaction at the thought of her carrying his child.

That scared the hell out of him. So did the notion that after just one night with her he didn't recognize himself.

Yet neither thought was as alarming as the realization that far from having his appetite appeased by the hours they'd just spent together, he still wanted her. Maybe even more than he had before.

Beside him, she shifted. Unable to help himself, he stroked his hand over the warm curve of her back, and in the next instant her breathing changed. With an instinct he didn't question, he knew she was awake.

Confirmation came half a dozen heartbeats later as she angled her head up to look at him. "John?" Her voice was a whisper, designed not to wake him if he were asleep.

"Yeah."

"What time is it?"

"A little past twelve."

"Ah." She pushed her hair off her face and settled back against him, resting her cheek against the slope of his shoulder. "Have you been awake long?"

"A while."

"I hope…" She fell silent, and then her breath sighed out. "I hope you haven't been lying here regretting what happened."

It was the perfect opening. All he had to do was claim that that was exactly what he was doing and that would be the end of it. Yet even as the thought entered his mind, he knew he wasn't going to do it. For a number of reasons, one of which was the hint of vulnerability he could hear in her voice. "No. I'm not sorry, Eve. But it does complicate things."

"Only if we let it."

He ignored the heat that coiled low in his stomach as her hand drifted over his hipbone. "You want to clarify that?"

"We're both adults. Why can't we agree not to make this complicated? To just…take it as it comes?"

He frowned. It was exactly what he'd been about to suggest. So why did the sound of it coming from her make him feel oddly dissatisfied? "It's not that simple."

"Why not?"

"It's just…not," he said, knowing he was being unreasonable but impatient at being pressed.

There was a long stretch of silence. Finally, in an exceedingly reasonable voice she said, "All right."

To his shock, she lifted her head off his shoulder and her hand off his stomach and sat up.

"What are you doing?" he demanded, coming upright himself as he felt the mattress give and realized she must have swung her legs over the edge of the bed.

"I'm going to my room." In contrast to his, her voice was soft.

"Why?"

"Because somehow I doubt you're about to propose. And if you don't want to just take things as they come, and you won't talk to me, that leaves us nothing, and I prefer to go without being asked."

He swore under his breath, wondering how he could have forgotten, even for a moment, her Chandler pride. "Damn it, Eve, don't."

"Don't what?"

"Don't make this harder than it is. I didn't mean we should break things off now. It's just—there are some issues we need to consider."

"Such as?"

"There's Lissy, for one. I wouldn't want her to get the wrong idea."

Slowly, she turned to face him. "Neither would I. I understand the need for discretion, John. I wouldn't be comfortable any other way."

"That's fine. But you also need to understand up-

front that I don't intend to make any long-term promises.''

"I'm not looking for promises," she said, still in
that same, quiet voice. "These past few months...I've
just started to learn the importance of living life on
my own terms. I'm not interested in seeing that
change.''

He told himself—again—that he ought to be glad
she valued her independence. After all, he'd had some
experience with women wanting to stake a claim on
him and he knew just how unpleasant things could get
when one party wanted more than the other was willing—or able—to give.

So why, just for a second, did some perverse little
part of him wish she were just a shade less reasonable,
a touch less self-contained?

He didn't know. But this clearly wasn't the time to
dwell on it. "All right. If you're sure you can handle
it."

As if on cue, beyond the night-dark windows the
moon suddenly slid free of the clouds, painting the
room with enough silvery light that he could see her
nod of consensus.

He could also see her full mouth and patrician features, the slender curve of her arms and shoulders, the
rounded breasts with their small, rose-colored nipples.
A drumbeat of need shuddered through him, gaining
strength as she raised her chin and her rain-gray gaze
met his.

He reached out and stroked his thumb lightly across
her cheek, down the sensitive line of her jaw, over that
delicate but determined chin. "Come back to bed."

She made a soft, needy sound. Parting her lips, she

caught his finger lightly between her teeth, then closed her lips around it.

His body rioted. Yet even as he pulled her into his arms, a part of him warned that he was making a mistake. He could kid himself all he wanted, it whispered, but the truth was he wanted more from Eve than just sex.

He pushed the thought away.

Seven

"Look, Eve! Look at me! I'm not falling off or anything!" Her two neat pigtails bouncing wildly, Lissy grinned as she circled the corral on Clue at a gentle trot.

Eve smiled back from her stance in the corral's center, making a small circle of her own on foot to keep the child in view. "You're doing great. Now sit down deeper in the saddle, ease back on the reins and tell her to walk, okay?"

Lissy pursed her lips in concentration and followed instructions, rewarded as the mare instantly eased into the slower gait. She glanced over again, her eyes gleaming with satisfaction. "How's that?"

"Perfect. Now why don't you turn around and try it in the other direction?"

"Can I canter after that?"

Eve swallowed a spurt of amusement. It hadn't

taken the little girl long to discover that it was much easier to keep her seat at the faster pace. "Yes."

"Good." Always eager to please, Lissy dutifully turned the horse and gave her the signal to trot.

Eve followed her progress, enjoying the pale October sun warming the top of her head and the sweet Montana air in her lungs. With a touch of surprise, she realized she felt relaxed, a minor miracle given that the last seven days had forever changed her view of the world, not to mention her image of herself.

She now knew that with the right man she was more than capable of being carried away by passion. That with just a look, a word, a single touch, she could be transformed into a woman who was openly needy and thoroughly wanton.

It was as heady as it was unsettling. Yet she took comfort in the knowledge that John seemed every bit as affected by her as she was by him. More than once this week she'd looked up in the middle of the day from some household chore to find him standing in the doorway. And no matter how valid his reason for being there, whether it was to grab his cell phone, change his shirt or get a bite to eat, he eventually found an excuse to touch her. And then one thing would lead to another....

She shivered with remembered pleasure, even as she acknowledged that like most things in life, it didn't come without a price. Hers was the growing awareness that when it came to living in the moment, the reality was considerably more difficult than the theory.

She blamed John for that. Because, as the week had unfolded, he'd not only proven to be a powerful, inventive lover, but had unwittingly revealed that there was a tender side to his nature, an unspoken need to be close directly at odds with his outward remoteness.

And it intrigued her, making her wonder what would happen if his guard ever truly came down. More times than she could count during the past days, she'd found herself not just thinking about him, but tempted to seek him out.

Not that she had any intention of giving into such desires. They'd agreed to take things easy, not to press, for one thing. For another, she was finally taking care of herself, making her own way in the world, and she was determined to keep it that way. She didn't want to make the mistake of depending on someone else for her happiness.

She also hadn't forgotten her vow to help Lissy. While things between father and daughter had already improved simply because John had been home more lately, he rarely took any initiative with the child. Eve knew it was ridiculous, but if it wasn't so at odds with his forceful personality, she'd swear he was afraid of saying or doing the wrong thing. Particularly since she'd now caught him several times watching Lissy with the sort of pained longing she'd first observed from the hallway last Friday night.

On the far side of the corral, Lissy brought Clue to a walk. "Eve?"

"Hmm?"

"What do you think my dad's gonna say when he sees me?"

"I don't know, sweetheart. But I think we're about to find out." Shading her eyes, she nodded toward the familiar black pickup coming lickety-split down the drive. "It looks like he got done checking out the truck Mr. Hansen has for sale sooner than he expected."

"But he can't do that!" Lissy wailed, staring in dismay at the swiftly approaching vehicle. "I'm not ready!"

Eve walked over to where the horse and rider had come to an abrupt halt. She gave the youngster's leg a reassuring squeeze. "Lissy, relax. You know what you're doing. And your dad *is* going to be pleased. I promise."

The child stared intently at Eve. Then, as if gaining strength from the conviction in her eyes, she took a deep breath and nodded. "Okay."

"Now, come on. Let's go say hello." With one last reassuring pat, she began to walk toward the fence, Lissy trailing behind her.

Tall and commanding, John climbed out of the pickup. His laser blue gaze found Eve, lingered for the merest moment, then shifted to Lissy. For a second his whole body stilled.

The child waved and urged the pinto forward. "Look, Daddy! It's me! I'm riding!"

"I'll be damned. You sure are." He headed in her direction as Eve slipped through the gate and walked around to join him at the fence.

Lissy's tentative smile grew a little brighter. "Are you surprised?"

"Absolutely."

She glanced at Eve, who gave her a nod of encouragement. "Do—do you want to see all the things I can do?"

"Sure."

Taking a deep breath, she straightened her narrow shoulders and carefully turned the pinto. After walking for a few paces along the fence, she nudged the animal into a trot.

John watched silently, but Eve didn't miss the way he drew himself up when Lissy momentarily lost her balance and slid sideways. "You sure this is wise?" he said abruptly.

Despite his brusqueness, she heard the concern in his voice. "Don't worry. She's fine."

As if on cue, the child settled more firmly into the saddle and some of the tension left John's posture. Propping an arm on the top of the fence, he looked over at Eve. "How long has this been going on?"

"A few weeks."

His eyes narrowed thoughtfully. "So that night in my study, when you asked about a horse to ride...?"

"It was for Lissy," she said easily, shifting her gaze back to her charge.

For the space of several long seconds she could feel him staring at her, but finally he, too, turned his attention to his daughter. "Yeah, well...you did all right."

"Thanks. But Lissy's the one who deserves the credit. She's worked hard to get over her fear of horses."

"I can see that." Uncharacteristically, he hesitated. "Did I forget to mention that I'm proud of her?"

John so rarely shared his thoughts or emotions that Eve felt oddly touched, as well as happy for Lissy. Without thinking, she reached out and squeezed his forearm. "I'm glad."

For a moment he seemed startled. Then he shrugged one big shoulder—but not before she saw the faint tide of color beneath his tan. The sight made her feel curiously off balance, and it was a relief when Lissy suddenly called her name.

"Eve? Can I canter now?"

"Go ahead." She watched as the child set the pinto

into a rocking-horse lope, making a circuit of the ring, giving Eve the time to gather her composure before she addressed John again. "You're back early. What did you think of Hansen's truck? Is it what you're looking for?"

"I don't know. It wasn't there."

"What happened?"

"Hansen's son broke his ankle skateboarding. So Hansen took his wife and the kid—and the truck—into town to the clinic."

"Oh. That's too bad. Is the boy going to be all right?"

"As far as I know. Hansen left word asking me to come back tomorrow." He frowned, rubbing his thumb over a nail protruding slightly from the fence post. "I know it's your day off, but I thought maybe you and Lissy might want to ride along. Afterward, we could grab a bite to eat."

She blinked, taken aback at the unexpected invitation. "I'm sorry, John, but I can't," she said with genuine regret. "Chrissy called earlier and asked me if I'd go to Missoula with her tomorrow, and I said I would."

Just for a second something flashed across his face that seemed to be as much displeasure as disappointment. Yet when he spoke, there was no sign of it in his voice. "I see. Maybe another time."

That was all there was time for as Lissy rode up. Bringing the pinto to a shambling stop, the child stared eagerly at her father. "Did you see me?"

"Yeah, I did." A little stiffly, he inclined his head. "That was real nice, Lis."

"Oh." Although she did her best to hide it, the child's whole body sagged at his lackluster praise.

Eve couldn't believe it. And she could see by John's suddenly taut expression that he knew he'd blown it. Wondering how such an intelligent man could miss the need to be more effusive when dealing with a child, she decided it was past time to give him a nudge in the right direction. "It *was* nice," she said warmly to Lissy. "As a matter of fact, your dad was just telling me how proud of you he is."

Lissy's gaze shot from her to John. "You were?"

Clearly aware he'd just been given a second chance, he said forcefully, "Yeah, I was. I *am*. A lot. You've worked real hard and it shows."

"Oh." The child's small face flushed with unmistakable pleasure.

There was a brief silence that might have grown awkward if Eve hadn't again interceded. "You know, sweetie, it's about time for me to get up to the house and get dinner started. So why don't you give Clue a good walk to cool her down and then take her on into the barn."

The youngster made a slight face. "Do I have to?"

"'Fraid so."

"Okay." With one last shy smile at her father, she turned the mare around and the two of them ambled off.

John watched her walk away. Not until she was all the way across the corral did he finally glance at Eve. "Thanks," he said simply.

She smiled. "It's not that hard, you know. If you'd loosen up a little and just talk to her, she'd do the rest."

He looked singularly unconvinced. "Yeah. I suppose."

She considered him for a moment, knowing he

probably wouldn't like what she was about to say, but was compelled to say it anyway. "About tomorrow…"

There was a glimmer of something that looked almost like hope on his face. "Yeah?"

"If you're just going to go off and leave her, I can take her with me."

For a moment he looked as if he wasn't sure he'd heard her right, and then his expression closed. "No. It's your day off. We'll manage." He glanced quickly at his watch. "I've got a sick heifer I need to check. I'll see you at dinner."

Eve couldn't decide if she felt pleased or exasperated at his answer. Before she could decide, he turned, strode over to his pickup, climbed in and roared off.

But suddenly she was glad that she'd accepted Chrissy's invitation. Not only would it be good for John and Lissy to spend some time alone together, but she clearly needed to get away. Because, despite her every intention to keep things simple, it was time she faced the truth.

Her feelings for John were far from casual.

Seated at the counter, John looked up from the Sunday paper as Eve walked into the kitchen the next morning. "You taking off?"

She opened her purse and began to rummage around inside. "Uh-huh."

He struggled to keep a scowl off his face. Dressed in slim black slacks and a pale pink twinset, with her hair done up in a French twist and a sleek black leather coat over her arm, she looked beautiful and sophisticated. Perfect for Paris, he thought sourly. All wrong for Missoula.

"There." Car keys in hand, she slipped the strap of her purse over her shoulder and smiled. "I guess I'll see you later. Be good, Lis," she called to the child, who was sitting on the floor in front of the TV set, quietly watching cartoons.

"I will," the little girl answered.

"Have a nice time," John murmured, turning his attention back to the paper. He sensed her gaze on him but he didn't look up. A few seconds later he heard the back door slap shut in her wake.

Released from the need for pretense, he pushed the paper aside and scowled, asking himself what the hell his problem was.

Unfortunately for his peace of mind, he knew.

It was Eve. God knew, he didn't begrudge her some time off; she worked hard and she deserved it. And he sure didn't expect her to double-check her every move with him, any more than he wanted her to seek him out every time she had a free moment.

But that didn't mean she had to take off to do the devil knew what with that airhead Chrissy Abrams. The two of them had been hell on wheels in high school, and he had no reason to think anything had changed now.

Yeah, that's right. Just think of all the trouble they can get into in Missoula on a Sunday. Why don't you admit it, MacLaren? The reason you're fried is because she made plans and they didn't include you.

He stood up abruptly and walked around into the kitchen to refresh his coffee. His movements were jerky as he told himself that last thought wasn't true and the contents of the pot splashed, stinging his hand. He swore.

"Daddy?"

Lissy's hesitant inquiry intruded on his unsettled thoughts. *"What?"*

"Is—is something the matter?"

He glanced impatiently at her, about to snap *no* when the apprehension in her eyes registered.

A wave of indignation shot through him, directed at himself. No matter how out of sorts he felt, it was no excuse for taking it out on his kid. He blew out a pent-up breath and did his best to wipe the scowl off his face. "Everything's fine. I just burned myself, that's all."

"Oh." Her big blue eyes studied him closely. "You know what?" Glancing away, she made a circle on the floor with one dainty finger.

He braced. "No. What?"

"I'm hungry."

Relief washed through him. "Okay. What are you hungry for?"

She looked up. "Pancakes."

Well, hell. That's what he got for asking. Cereal would at least be quick and easy. Ditto toast or your basic fried egg. Pancakes, however, took time. And with Lissy, time was always his enemy, stretching interminably as he struggled to behave like a proper father.

"I could help," she offered, clearly misunderstanding his silence. "I know how 'cause I help Eve all the time, even though she's a really good cook."

The ingenuous comment served to stiffen his spine. "All right."

"Really?"

"Yeah."

It was all the encouragement she needed. Leaping to her feet, she came around the end of the counter, darted into the pantry and emerged lugging a large yellow box of pancake mix. "It tells you how to make them right here," she explained, scooting up next to him and indicating the back panel.

"I know how to make pancakes."

"You do?"

He took the box from her. "Yeah."

"Oh."

Oddly enough, she looked crestfallen. Puzzled, John couldn't imagine what the problem was—until it dawned on him that her offer to help had been more than a mere courtesy.

Great. They'd been together all of five minutes and already he'd screwed that up. Frustrated, he tried to think of something he could say to retrieve the situation, but typically, the words refused to come.

"Daddy?"

"What?"

"I could get a mixing bowl for you. That is, if you want me to. I know right where Eve keeps them." She stared up earnestly at him, her expression an odd combination of resolve and uncertainty.

"Well, yeah. That'd be nice."

"Okay!" Just like that, she scampered happily toward the cupboard, smiling back at him over her shoulder. "Do you want me to get the eggs and the milk, too?"

"Sure." Bemused by her eagerness, he forced his gaze away from her innocent face and considered the back of the pancake box. He wasn't quite sure what had just happened, but he was grateful for it nevertheless.

Lissy set the bowl on the counter with a clatter. "Daddy?"

"Huh?"

"If you really know how to make pancakes, how come you're reading the directions?"

He started to shrug the question off with a noncommittal answer, then remembered Eve's admonition to loosen up. "Because I haven't done this since I was a teenager," he said, mentally cutting the recipe in half. "And then I was cooking for a dozen guys with big appetites."

"Oh." There was a slight pause. When she spoke again, her voice held a note of awe. "I guess that means you have lots and lots of brothers, huh?"

As the question sank in, he realized what he'd revealed and was appalled. Normally, he didn't talk about his childhood. With anyone. Yet as he glanced over and found her looking at him with open curiosity, he knew he couldn't let her think she had other family when she didn't. "They weren't my brothers."

A little V formed between her eyebrows. "They weren't?"

"No." He opened the cupboard and got out the measuring cups. "You know what an orphan is?"

She nodded.

"That's what I was. I lived with a bunch of other boys in a group home about fifty miles from here."

"Oh." There was a heartbeat of silence. "Who took care of you?"

"Different people. It changed over the years." Having already said more than he wanted to, he took a stab at changing the subject. "So. You gonna get the rest of the stuff for the batter or not?"

"Oh—oh, yeah!"

To his relief, she took the hint and bolted toward the refrigerator. In need of a moment to regroup, he retrieved the griddle and turned it on to heat. He was just beginning to feel more at ease when the refrigerator door slammed and he glanced over to see her clutching a gallon container of milk to her chest with one hand while gripping the basket holding the eggs with the other.

Off balance, she started toward him. His heart kicked into overdrive as her stocking feet slid precariously on the polished stone floor. "Damn it, Lissy, slow down!"

The instant he said it, even before she jolted to a stop and he saw the pink climb into her cheeks, he regretted it. Not the sentiment, perhaps, but the swear word, his harsh voice, his overbearing manner—and, most of all, his certainty that he'd just ruined an encounter that for once had seemed to be going right.

Angry at himself, he said curtly, "Look, I'm sorry. I shouldn't have snapped at you. But I was afraid you were going to fall and I didn't want you to get hurt, all right?"

To his amazement, instead of shrinking away she stared right back at him, the oddest expression on her face. "You didn't?"

He shook his head. "No."

"Oh." For a moment she almost appeared to brighten, and it seemed as if things were going to be all right. And then she suddenly bit her lower lip. "Daddy?"

His heart sank. "What?"

"Can you take the milk? It's heavy."

He closed the distance between them with a single step, took both food items and set them on the counter. "That better?"

She nodded. "Uh-huh. Only…"

"What?"

"Can I pour the batter when it's ready?"

In that instant, as he met the big blue eyes gazing steadily up at him, he finally saw what had been staring him in the face for the past two weeks. She'd changed. A month ago she would have bolted for her room at his first harsh word. But not anymore. Like a flower that was finally taking root, she was blossoming with newfound trust and confidence.

And he knew exactly who was to thank.

He cleared his throat. "Sure. Just let me grab the step stool—" suiting action to words, he dragged it out of the corner and set it by the counter with a clatter "—and you can help me make it."

Her eyes widened. "Really?"

"Yeah. Only take your socks off first."

"Okay!" She tore them off in a flash and clambered up beside him as if fearing he'd change his mind.

Taking turns measuring and pouring, they put the batter together. When it was ready, he pushed the bowl toward her and handed her a measuring cup. "You know what to do?"

"Uh-huh." She dipped the cup in the batter. Then she carefully lifted it up and poured a succession of lopsided circles onto the griddle.

"Pretty good," he murmured.

As compliments went, it wasn't much. Even so, her face lit up. The sight made him feel funny, and he shifted his gaze to the pancakes rising on the griddle, only to stiffen in surprise as she took a half step sideways and tentatively leaned her weight against him.

He tried to decide what to do. Yet it didn't take him more than a few seconds to realize he'd never forgive himself if she were to overbalance and topple off the stool. Gingerly, he settled her more securely into the crook of his arm.

She gave a contented little sigh. "Daddy?"

"Hmm?"

"I'm glad I'm not an orphan."

He kept his gaze firmly fixed on the rising pancakes, his throat suddenly tight. "Yeah. Me, too."

To his relief, his voice sounded steady and matter of fact. Yet for the very first time since Lissy had come to live with him, he felt a kernel of hope that there might be hope for him as a father after all.

Eight

"Lissy looks happy tonight," Pam Abrams said to Eve.

The teacher's low voice carried easily despite the din in Lander County Elementary's second-grade classroom, which was filled with kids and parents all gussied up for the school's annual fall parents' night.

"Yes, she does," Eve agreed, following the other woman's gaze across the room to where the child stood beside her tall, broad-shouldered father.

Something good was happening between John and his daughter. Eve had suspected as much all week. Although the changes had been subtle, John seemed to be a little more at ease, a little less aloof with the child than he had been in the past.

His behavior tonight was a case in point. Instead of keeping Lissy at arm's length, he'd devoted the evening to her, touring the classroom, inspecting her desk, listening attentively as she talked about what she most and least liked to study. While not everything had been clear sailing—John had looked distinctly uncomfortable when they'd first walked in and half a dozen giggling little girls had rushed over to say hello to Lissy—he seemed to be making a genuine effort.

The result could be seen in the happy glow on Lissy's face. Dressed in a fashionable pink jumper, worn with a lace-trimmed white T-shirt, white tights and pink tennis shoes, with her perky golden-brown curls caught off her face with a quintet of little pink butterfly clips, she bore scant resemblance to the bedraggled, sad-eyed little waif of a month ago.

Nor was Eve the only one to think so, as Pam soon made clear. "She's come a long way in the past month," the teacher commented. "She's lucky to have you."

"I'm the lucky one," Eve replied, knowing it was true. Above and beyond providing her with food in her mouth and a roof over her head, her job taking care of Lissy had given her a purpose. For the first time in years she felt useful, as though she were making a small but worthwhile difference in the world, and it felt good.

Perhaps that was why she felt no sense of foreboding as Pam walked away to greet another set of parents and Gus Bolt, the bespectacled young Lander attorney who'd handled the Rocking C's sale, approached.

"Eve. Nice to see you."

"Hello, Gus."

"I understand from Freddy—" he indicated one of Lissy's classmates, a thin, dark-haired little boy who was his spitting image "—that you've been helping in the classroom. I'm glad to see things are working out."

"Thank you." Bolt's gaze shifted momentarily and she turned to see John approaching. His eyes met hers for a moment as he stepped up beside her, before he turned his attention to the shorter, slighter man.

"Gus, you know John MacLaren, don't you?" she said easily.

"Of course." The two men shook hands and exchanged greetings.

Once the amenities were out of the way, Bolt's attention swung back to her. "I tried calling you earlier this evening, but apparently you'd already left for town." Again his gaze flickered to John, then came back to her. "Can you give me a call tomorrow? Something's come up that I need to discuss with you."

She hesitated, her curiosity piqued. "Surely you can give me a hint?" she said wryly. "John knows why I had to sell the ranch."

"In that case…I'm afraid I've been contacted by yet another gentleman claiming he had dealings with Max."

Her amusement died. "Oh."

"This one's name is Morris Chapman. He's from New Mexico, says he just learned of Max's passing and claims he has something important to discuss with you. Naturally, I explained I was handling matters and refused to give out your phone number. Unfortunately, that seemed to get his dander up and he said he'd be sending you some papers. I thought you might know who he is."

She shook her head, filled with dismay at the prospect of dealing with yet another creditor. Gamely, she tried to rise above it, but some of her distress must have shown on her face, as evidenced by the attorney's quick look of concern.

"I'm sorry, Eve. But I did warn you this was a possibility when you decided to use your personal assets to settle those last liabilities."

Beside her, she felt John stiffen and abruptly realized she'd never thought to correct his initial impression that she'd squandered all her money on herself.

Gus reached out and gave her hand a quick squeeze. "I debated whether to say anything until I have a better idea what's involved, but decided it would be best if you were prepared."

"Of course, Gus. You were right to tell me."

The attorney visibly relaxed and they spent the next few minutes discussing how well young Freddy was doing in school before he excused himself and went off in search of his wife and son.

Bracing herself, she turned to John. To her surprise, though there was speculation in his eyes, after a quick look around he seemed to decide this was not the right time to pursue answers. Instead, he said quietly, "You all right?"

Relieved, she smiled. "I'm fine."

"Good."

She looked around. "Where's Lissy?"

He nodded toward the cloakroom as she and three other little girls, including her best friend Jenny, emerged, chattering excitedly as they shrugged into their coats. "The Hendersens are getting ready to leave."

"Already?" Lissy was going home with Kristin Hendersen, who was having a slumber party; John and Eve had dropped her things off earlier on the drive into town.

"It's nearly nine o'clock."

"Oh." She stared at him in amazement, surprised at how fast the evening had gone. In the next instant Lissy came skipping up to say goodbye and to confide that she and her friends were going to stay up "really, really late" so they weren't to come get her before noon. John nodded, Eve told her not to worry, and a moment later she was gone.

There was a moment's silence following the child's departure. Then John's gaze found Eve's, and the banked heat she could see in those deep blue depths set off a throb of need inside her. "Let's go home," he said abruptly.

"All right." She went and got her coat, exquisitely aware of the light touch of his hand at the small of her back as they said their goodbyes and walked out of the school.

The October night was crisp and clear. Stars twinkled like silver sequins against the ebony fabric of the sky, their pale, shimmering light unaffected by the thin slice of an ivory moon.

Eve looked out at the familiar landscape and drank in the silence, awed by the vast beauty of the land, wondering how she could have stayed away as long as she had. With the sort of understanding that comes with hindsight, she realized the restlessness she'd felt so often the past few years had actually been homesickness. While she refused to regret those years, knowing they'd taught her a lot, she was glad to be home.

"You're awfully quiet."

John's deep voice brought her head around. She allowed herself a moment to appreciate his chiseled profile, illuminated by the dashboard lights. "So are you."

A faint smile curved his chiseled mouth. "I guess I am."

That unexpected smile made her feel warm all over. "I was just thinking about all the parties I used to attend and wondering how I stood all the noise."

"Don't you miss it?"

"The noise?"

He shot her a chiding look. "No. The parties. And the travel, the glamorous people, not having any responsibilities?"

She laughed softly. "No. I had fun, and I saw a lot of beautiful places, but this is where I belong. I just wish I'd figured it out before I lost Granddad. I keep thinking that maybe, if I'd come home, I could have done something to help him."

He shook his head. "Don't kid yourself, Eve. I liked your grandfather, but he'd been in charge too many years to suddenly relinquish his authority. Not to mention he was a proud man. He would've hated having you know he was in trouble."

Although she'd told herself the very same thing, the conviction in John's voice was strangely comforting. "I know you're right. But sometimes it's just...hard."

He nodded. "Yeah," he said quietly. "I suppose it is."

The understanding in his voice surprised her. Feeling closer to him than she ever had before, she asked, "Did you have a good time tonight?"

"I'm not sure a good time is exactly how I'd phrase it but, yeah, I did. Lis seems to like school. I'm glad she's doing well."

"What about you? Did you like school?"

He shrugged. "It was all right."

"I imagine it was hard, not having anyone to call your own."

He hesitated. And then, just when she'd decided he wasn't going to answer, he surprised her. "Yeah, it was. Kids don't like being different. Sometimes I used to wonder..."

"What?"

"Just...why me? But I got over it. I survived." John suddenly heard what he'd just said and grimaced. The last thing he wanted was her pity, and he deliberately changed the subject. "What did Bolt mean when he said you'd used your personal assets to settle some of Max's liabilities?"

"It's nothing."

"It's not nothing. I want to know."

She hesitated, as if weighing her answer, but finally gave a faint sigh, as if she knew he had no intention of letting it go. "After the rest of the creditors made their claims, there wasn't enough money left to pay the Rocking C's hands their back wages. I took care of that and a few other things."

"You took care of it," he repeated slowly, his mind working. "With what? The money from your trust fund?"

"Yes."

"Back wages took all of it?"

"Granddad hadn't paid payroll taxes for nearly two years. What with interest and penalties, it added up. And as trustee, he had the power to make investments." She paused and in the glow from the dashboard, he saw her shrug. "Some of them weren't very wise."

John felt something inside him shift as he listened

to her answer, which was notable for its lack of self-pity. Almost reluctantly, he admitted that despite the growing evidence to the contrary, up until tonight a part of him had continued to regard her as the spoiled, pampered princess he'd labeled her eight years ago. And though he tried to tell himself he wasn't sure why, on some level he knew it had to do with the unwelcome discovery that she was starting to feel important to him.

Not that he was falling in love with her or anything as foolish as that, he told himself firmly. Or that it would change anything if he did. He still wasn't suited for family life, or for the intimacy demanded by marriage.

It was just that he didn't like the idea of Eve worrying about money. And he did have a responsibility toward her. She was his employee, as well as his lover, and that meant he had an obligation to see to her welfare.

"I don't want you to worry about this new claim, if that's what it turns out to be," he said decisively.

"What do you mean?"

"Whatever this guy from New Mexico wants, I'll handle it."

"Pardon me?"

"I said, I'll handle it." He slowed and took the turn onto the Bar M road.

For a handful of seconds she seemed stunned. "That's very generous," she said finally. "But I couldn't possibly accept. It's my problem and I'll take care of it."

"Damn it, Eve—"

She leaned over and touched her hand to his arm to silence him. "John, please. I don't expect you to understand, but for so long I did whatever was easiest. Being responsible for myself is important to me. And I really don't want to argue about this.'' Her voice dropped even further, taking on a slightly husky note. ''Not tonight.''

Her touch was like a brand, making his blood heat, while that velvety voice stroked along his senses. She was such a contradiction, stubbornly independent one minute, a warm, yielding temptress the next. Although they'd been as intimate as a man and a woman could be the past pair of weeks, he still didn't quite know what to expect, a realization he found more than a little frustrating.

But then, he'd had a crash course in frustration lately. It had been more than a week since they'd last made love; first Lissy had been home with a cold, then Eve had spent the bulk of the remaining days at school helping Miss Abrams and the kids get ready for tonight.

And when they had made love, they'd been under a time constraint, forced by Lissy's schedule, Eve's obligations and his own work demands to limit their time together. Add to that the fact that his self-control seemed to be on a permanent vacation, that no matter how often he told himself he was going to take it slow there always came a moment when wildfire need overcame his formerly effortless self-discipline, and it was no wonder he felt edgy.

Nor had his state of mind been helped by the way she was dressed tonight, in thin, strappy high heels and a simple but elegant navy silk dress that had been driving him crazy since they'd left home three hours ago.

Still, he promised himself this subject wasn't over

even as he outwardly acquiesced. "All right. We'll drop it for now."

"Good."

He pulled up to the house and cut the pickup's engine, frowning as he saw that the porch light was out. "Stay put," he ordered as she reached for her door handle. Undoing his seat belt, he climbed out, went around, opened her door, leaned in and scooped her into his arms.

"John!" she protested, her hands locking around his neck for balance. "What do you think you're doing?"

He straightened and bumped the door closed with his hip. "It's dark out here. I don't want to take a chance on you falling in those heels." Only to himself did he admit that he simply couldn't wait to hold her a second longer.

Her body felt sleek and supple against his as he strode across the yard and up the steps, while her light, powdery scent teased at his senses. Stopping at the door, he gave in to temptation, lifted her higher and lowered his head as the desire he'd been keeping so tightly leashed broke free.

His mouth settled over hers, hot and demanding. To his gratification, her lips immediately parted, clinging hungrily to his. With a sweetly satisfying moan, she tightened her arms around his neck and twisted closer.

John drank in the taste of her, his body tight with need. In the back of his mind, he marveled at her powerful effect on him, which seemed to be growing rather than diminishing with time. Marveled, and felt the tiniest spark of alarm...

He broke the seal of their lips and set her on her feet, gritting his teeth as she leaned against him and he felt the slim, elegant curves of her body. He allowed himself the indulgence of rubbing his cheek against the fragrant silk of her pale hair before he straightened. "Come on. Let's go inside."

Keeping her close, he opened the door and ushered her in, their path illuminated by the soft glow of light from the kitchen. With a touch of his hand to her shoulder, he guided her through the house and down the hall to his bedroom.

He snapped on the bedside lamp and reached for her, pulling her close for another hungry kiss. By the time he raised his head, they were both breathing hard. Taking a firm grip on himself, he took her purse and helped her out of her coat, shed his own and tossed everything onto the big upholstered chair that took up most of one corner. Moments later, the rest of his clothing followed, until he was standing before her unabashedly naked. "Turn around," he said softly.

Her wide gray eyes searched his for a moment, then swept slowly downward, a faint flush of color rising in her cheeks at the proof of his desire jutting thickly from his body. For a moment he thought she was going to balk at his request, and then she dampened her lips and did as he bid.

Slowly, he unzipped her dress, exposing the silky line of her back, bare except for the coffee-colored lace of her bra and panties. Brushing her hair out of his way, he bent his head and pressed his mouth to her nape, stringing a chain of kisses a few inches down her spine.

"John," she protested weakly.

"Shh." He pushed her dress off her shoulders, feeling a distinct throb in his groin as it slid to the floor and he saw that her nylons came only to the tops of her thighs, held there by built-in lace bands. The sight of her smooth, bare legs rising out of them made his whole body go hard. "It's been a hell of a long week," he ground out, his breathing suddenly labored. "I missed touching you." He unclipped her bra, pushed it off her arms, and reached around to cup her breasts in his palms.

"Oh." Eve gasped, squeezing her eyes shut as he traced the shape of her tightly beaded nipples with the broad tips of his fingers while blazing a trail along the sensitive underside of her jaw with his mouth. Sensation streaked through her, hot and melting. Her knees felt weak, her body heavy.

She leaned back against John's big, hard frame. At moments like this she was acutely aware of the difference in their size and strength. And yet she felt no fear, but rather a delicious sense of her own femininity. There was no question that he was uncompromisingly, overwhelmingly male, but she trusted him to use all that raw, masculine power for her pleasure.

His right hand drifted down her midsection and over the satin of her panties, coming to rest between her legs. With wicked accuracy, he honed in with his thumb and began to stroke her.

Her whole body flushed. Pleasure twisted through her, stealing her breath, making her rock her hips in time to the rhythm he set. It was too much and not enough all at the same time. Needing more, she reached up, twined her fingers in the cool, black satin of his hair and tugged down his head to claim his mouth.

Lips parted, they kissed, tongues tangled, breath intermixed. With every brush of his hand, tension climbed higher inside her. Just when she was sure she couldn't take any more, his fingers paused, lifted, then skated beneath her panties and slid over her damp, aching cleft.

She tore her mouth from his. "John. Oh, oh please!" She came up on tiptoe, quivering as she felt the rigid weight of his sex nudging heavily into her back, the sure press of one fingertip at her opening. "I need, I want…"

"What?" His voice was raw, his touch sure and skilled as it slid over her, setting her on fire. "What do you need, Eve?"

"You. I need you."

A shudder went through him and the breath hissed out between his teeth. The next thing she knew he was turning her around, lifting her out of the pool of her dress and backing toward the bed, where he sank down with her standing between his thighs.

He cradled her hips in his hands, his fingers stroking the bare skin between her nylons and panties. "What the hell do you call these things, anyway?" he asked hoarsely, touching the elasticized tops of her hose.

She swallowed, searching to find her voice, no mean feat when her whole body ached for him. "Thigh-highs."

"Yeah? If I'd had any idea that's what you had on, we'd have been home a hell of a lot sooner." To her wonder, his hands shook slightly as he peeled her panties down her legs, leaving her in hose and heels and nothing else.

That telltale tremor in his big, competent hands made her bold. Trembling herself, she kicked off her shoes, stepped forward, locked her arms around his powerful neck and straddled his lap. He wrapped an arm around her waist and slowly began to guide himself inside her.

She rocked upward to accommodate him, squeezing her eyes shut at his unhurried entry, shuddering as he stroked his hand down her spine. Sensation overwhelmed her; the tantalizing brush of his hard warm chest against her breasts, the tickle of the hair on his legs between her thighs, the satin over steel play of flexing muscle as she braced her hands on his wide shoulders, the slow, heated pressure as he filled her.

"Eve." His voice whispered over her like rough velvet.

She opened her eyes and found herself transfixed by the intensity of his gaze.

John stared back, a fierce, totally male satisfaction filling him as they came together. He was acutely aware of the slenderness of her waist between his hands, the elegant fineness of her bones compared to his.

He knew, from a few things she'd said, that he was the first man to give her pleasure. Which seemed only fair, since she was the first woman for whom he'd experienced this all-consuming hunger. Each time he was with her he wanted more.

She moved, rocking upright, slowly sinking down, and he gave an unexpected groan, the sound torn from the very heart of him.

Satisfaction stole across her face. "Do you like that?"

"What do you think?" Although his body was already screaming for release, he fought the urge to grip her hips, to quicken the tempo, determined to let her set the pace.

Perspiration beaded his forehead as she did just that,

settling into a protracted rhythm that seemed guaranteed to drive him mad. Desperate for a diversion, he found her mouth with his own, but the sweetness of her lips as they parted for the hot slide of his tongue did nothing to relieve his building tension.

And then he heard her breathing quicken and felt her soft, inner muscles begin to tighten. Gritting his teeth against a rising flood of pleasure, he brought his hand around and lightly rubbed his fingertip over the swollen center of her desire.

She tore her mouth from his as her whole body shuddered. "Oh. Oh, John!" Sobbing, she clung to his shoulders as the velvet glove of her body clenched around him again and again. "Don't stop, don't stop!"

He couldn't hold back any longer. With a guttural cry of his own, he gripped her hips and drove into her, his back hollowing as his own pleasure slammed into him.

It was long minutes later before he found the strength to lift his head. Gathering her close, he twisted around and lay back on the bed with her sprawled against him. Her hand came up and stroked gently over his face, then her thumb feathered lightly over his parted lips.

A surge of possessiveness went through him and he reached up, caught her hand in his and kissed her palm. She was his. And while he might not be the marrying kind, neither did he have any intention of giving her up, not in the immediate future.

What's more, he intended to take care of her.

Whether she wanted him to or not.

The phone rang before dawn. Eve came awake long enough to hear the sharp concern in John's voice and to make sympathetic noises when he climbed out of bed and began to pull on his clothes, brusquely explaining that the call had been from one of his men reporting that his favorite gelding had gotten out of his stall and into the grain bin and appeared to be foundering.

The next thing she knew, the clock read five after nine, sunshine was streaming in the windows, and John still wasn't back.

She stretched, bunched the pillow under her head and turned onto her side, grimacing at the slight soreness in her thighs. Taking stock, she realized that the skin on her face and chest felt tender and her lips slightly swollen, but overall what she felt was a sort of bone-deep languor.

Which wasn't surprising since she and John had made love three times last night.

What was surprising was the discovery that he'd been gone only a few hours and she missed him.

She immediately told herself not to be foolish. Of course she missed him. She missed his embrace, and the hard strength of his body against hers and the chance to make love again before it was time to go get Lissy.

Yet it was more than that, and she knew it. She missed his deep voice. She missed lying quietly in bed and talking the way they'd talked last night. She missed his smile, the way his glorious blue eyes darkened when he looked at her and the sense of safety she felt when his arms were around her.

Suddenly restless, she tossed back the covers and climbed out of bed. Despite the sunshine, the early morning air felt cool against her bare skin. Rubbing her arms, she glanced at her wrinkled dress, but the idea of putting it on didn't appeal.

With sudden decision, she walked over to John's dresser, telling herself he wouldn't begrudge her a T-shirt. Trying not to feel as if she were prying, she began opening drawers. Her first forays yielded underwear, jeans and socks until finally she found a stack of cotton T-shirts.

Shivering now, she drew the top one off the stack and pulled it on, sighing as the soft cotton slid over her. Although it was probably her imagination, since the shirt was freshly laundered, she would have sworn she could smell John's scent. Hugging it to her, she leaned over to shut the drawer when a swatch of bright red cloth at the very back of the drawer caught her eye. Intrigued—she didn't think she'd ever seen him in a shirt that wasn't navy, black or plain white—she reached in and tugged the garment free, frowning as she realized it was wrapped in a thin layer of tissue paper.

The tissue fell away and she saw that the item wasn't a T-shirt at all, but a small child's faded corduroy jacket. For a moment she assumed it was Lissy's, but as she unfolded it she realized it was far too small and that the style had to be several decades old.

She stared at the small rectangle of paper pinned to the front with a large safety pin. The writing on it was faded but easy to read, done in the large, loopy handwriting so often favored by teenage girls.

His name is John. Tell him I loved him and I'm sorry, but I tried and I just can't take care of him.

Eve's heart seemed to still as she realized the coat must have been the one John had been wearing when he'd been abandoned as a little boy. That the note could only have been written by his mother. And that John—outwardly so tough and so very unsentimental—had kept the item all these years.

Emotion swept her. Heartache for the defenseless, innocent, no-doubt bewildered child he'd been. Pride for the hurdles he'd faced and the man he'd become. And, as she smoothed the thin paper with trembling fingers, carefully refolded the coat and replaced it in the drawer, a mixture of elation and dread.

Because as she slowly shut the drawer and straightened, she knew why she missed him and why she'd found such pleasure in his arms.

She loved him. It was probably a mistake and he'd probably break her heart, but she also knew that didn't matter.

She loved him, now and forever, with everything that was in her heart.

Nine

Eve pulled the heavy roasting pan out of the oven and set it on the larger of the two front burners. Lifting the lid, she inhaled the rich aroma of simmering meat and vegetables. Although the past few days had been sunny, the temperature had been falling steadily in the week and a half since the school open house, and the hot, savory meal seemed perfect for a chilly fall evening.

She turned up the heat on the oven and slid a pan of biscuits inside. Reaching to set the timer, she heard the back door slam and the approaching stamp of footsteps. A few seconds later, a familiar male voice said, "Whatever you're cooking, it sure smells good."

She looked over to see John lounging in the doorway, and her heart beat a little faster. Dressed in boots, jeans, a navy henley and a quilted black vest, his hair ruffled from the breeze and the day's beard shadowing his lean cheeks, he looked vital, virile, the quintessential male. "It's pot roast."

"Could've fooled me. It smells like heaven."

She smiled. "I take it you're hungry."

"Yeah. You could say that." His gaze met hers, and there was a spark in his eyes that suggested he wasn't talking only about food. "How are you?" he asked quietly. "And how'd it go with Lissy at Dr. Edger's?"

"I'm fine and so is she, although she wasn't very happy about having to get her finger pricked for the blood sample."

"Is everything all right?"

"Doc said she seems perfectly healthy. He signed her health card, and we dropped it off at the rec center on our way home." Much to Lissy's delight, one of the local guilds was offering a ballet class for kids age six to ten. "She can hardly wait. Especially since the teacher told her they're going to have a Christmas recital."

"That's great."

It was clear he meant it, and Eve felt a wave of tenderness go through her. Most of the men she knew would roll their eyes at the prospect of an evening spent watching a bunch of little girls twirl around a stage pretending to be snowflakes or sugar plums, but not John. He might not always know the right thing to say to Lissy or how to act, but there was no longer a single doubt in her mind that he genuinely cared about his daughter.

As if he'd read her mind, an uncharacteristic flash of self-consciousness registered on his face and he promptly changed the subject. "You hear anything from Bolt about that Chapman fellow?'' he asked a tad gruffly.

"No, not yet.''

"Huh.'' For a second she thought he was going to pursue it, but then he seemed to think better of it. "So how long until dinner?''

"I still have to make the gravy and set the table.'' She calculated. "Say, ten minutes?''

"I'll go wash up.''

She nodded and went to get the flour and an instant gravy packet out of the pantry as he walked away. Yet he remained the focus of her thoughts as she mixed the items together in a measuring cup, added water and stirred until smooth.

He'd changed. Granted, it was subtle, more a general easing of his manner than an actual shift in attitude, but he was different just the same. Overall, he seemed more relaxed and less guarded with both her and Lissy, and it made her happy. While she was doing her best to take things day by day, she couldn't deny that her heart felt a little fuller each time he revealed another facet of his complex personality.

Turning the heat on the burner to a medium temperature, she lifted the lid on the roasting pan and poured in the gravy mixture, blending it with the beef broth she'd added earlier to the roast's natural juices.

By the time the liquid started to bubble a few minutes later, John was back. This time he'd shed the vest and his sleeves were pushed back. Crossing the kitchen, he grabbed three of the place mats stacked in the middle of the table and set them in place. "Where is Lis, anyway?''

"In her room. She finished her homework right before you came in and went to put it away. She has a surprise for you.'' He glanced at her curiously, and she tried to look angelic. ''Sorry. I promised not to tell.'' Grabbing a hot pad as the buzzer rang, she retrieved the now golden biscuits and diplomatically changed the subject. ''How was your day?''

He came back around the counter and opened the silverware drawer. ''Productive. We moved the last group of stragglers down from Gull Creek, replaced a few tons of hay that went bad and got the last of the horses reshod.'' Gathering knives, forks, spoons and a trio of napkins, he headed back toward the table.

''Is that the farrier's rig that's parked out in the yard?'' The deluxe cherry-red sport-utility vehicle had been there when she'd returned from picking up Lissy at school. At the time she'd thought it was odd that it should be at the house rather than the barn, but then she'd promptly forgotten about it.

There was the slightest hesitation before he answered. ''No.''

''Oh. Well, whose is it?''

''Mine.''

She glanced over at him in surprise. ''You got rid of your pickup?''

''No.'' He put the last fork into place and turned to face her, anticipation suddenly lighting his deep blue eyes. ''I bought it for you to drive.''

For a moment she just stared at him. ''But it's brand-new!''

He gave one of those expressive shrugs she'd come to know so well. ''So? It's not like I can't afford it.''

''Well, yes, but...'' She broke off, suddenly realizing that if she wasn't careful she was going to hurt his feelings. ''I just...you shouldn't have. It's too much.''

Nobody's fool, his eyes narrowed. He studied her for a moment and when he spoke his voice had gone quiet. "What's the problem?"

It was a good question. Eve tried to decide how to explain her uneasiness. "I suppose," she said honestly, "it's a little like the coat—"

"Aw, hell." His frustration was obvious as he stalked back into the kitchen. "We're not going to get into that again, are we? You needed a decent winter coat instead of that thin little leather thing you've been wearing, so I bought you one. You insisted on paying me back out of your next few paychecks, and I agreed. End of story.

"As far as the Explorer's concerned, it's not the same at all," he went on. "The title's in my name. And one way or another I was going to have to replace the Wagoneer anyway." He let out a sigh and abruptly changed tactics. "The thing is fifteen years old, Eve," he said more reasonably. "It's fine for getting around the ranch, but the heater's not always reliable and the four-wheel drive doesn't always engage. What with the forecasters saying we may get snow by the weekend, and you driving back and forth to town as much as you do, I need to know that Lissy and you are safe."

It was hard to argue with that. Particularly when he'd actually made the effort to explain himself, which was a rarity in itself.

Besides, what exactly *was* she protesting? Yes, he'd bought her a beautiful coat. But in all fairness, at the time they'd been shopping for a new parka for Lissy, and it had been the child who'd insisted that Eve needed one, too. It wasn't as if John had intended to buy it for her when they'd set out. And, as he'd pointed out, the vehicle *was* in his name, and she could hardly fault him for being concerned about his daughter's safety.

This wasn't like the situation with Max, she assured herself. John wasn't trying to run her life or tell her what to do. Yes, he was looking out for her, but given her feelings, she'd do the same for him if he'd let her. Instead of complaining, she ought to be glad that he was concerned.

She slowly let out a breath and managed a smile. "You're right. I'm sorry. I just don't want you to think I expect you to buy me things."

"Believe me, I don't." Catching her off-guard, he leaned over and kissed her, softly at first, and then with more and more heat. By the time he raised his head, her breathing was shaky and her knees were weak.

He tucked a stray strand of hair behind her ear. "I think we'd better eat." His mouth twisted ruefully. "While we still can."

Lips tingling, she nodded and went to put dinner on the table.

Lissy's surprise for John turned out to be herself, decked out in tights, leotard and tutu. With her delicate torso and skinny legs, the large froth of yellow netting billowing around her middle made her look a lot like an overripe dandelion he decided as she twirled around the living room demonstrating her ballerina moves.

"Come on, kiddo, that's enough." Eve set the biscuits and a bowl of peaches next to the steaming platter of roast and vegetables and sat down at the table. "You're going to make yourself so dizzy you won't be able to eat."

Lissy slowly teetered to a stop. "Okay," she said breathlessly. Cheeks flushed, her hair a froth of curls, she swayed, then righted herself and headed for her place.

"Do you need to wash your hands?" Eve asked gently.

The little girl gave a gusty sigh. "Yeah, I s'pose." She trotted into the kitchen and gave herself a quick wash at the sink.

"You probably should take off your tutu," Eve suggested to her as she rejoined the adults.

"Do I have to?"

"No. But I don't think you want to take a chance on spilling anything on it, do you?"

Lissy considered, then quickly shook her head. She slipped the tutu off and carefully set it on one of the club chairs as Eve filled her plate.

The next few minutes were devoted to taking the edge off all their hunger. Like everything Eve cooked, the meal was delicious, John thought, as he swallowed a bite of moist, succulent beef.

"Guess what, Daddy?" Lissy looked over at him, her big blue eyes soft and trusting. "I got a hundred on my spelling test."

"Well, good for you."

"*And* Miss Abrams picked one of my pictures to go in Mr. Adams' showcase."

"Hey, that's great." Mr. Adams was the principal, and from parents' night John knew that it was an honor to have your work shown in the big glass display outside the school office.

"Uh-huh. Eve said I should be really proud of myself, didn't you, Eve?"

"I sure did."

Lissy beamed. "So I am."

John watched as the two females exchanged smiles, grateful for their obvious fondness of each other. He cleared his throat. "I understand you were a pretty brave girl at the doctor's today."

Lissy's brow crinkled. "I was?"

"For your blood test."

She instantly shook her head. "I was scared," she admitted guilelessly. "I cried and wouldn't put out my hand 'cause I was afraid it was going to hurt, but then Eve said they could do it to her first, and after that…it wasn't too bad."

His gaze flickered to Eve's hands, and for the first time he noticed the small adhesive strip adorning one of her fingertips.

He raised an eyebrow and she shrugged. "It seemed like the thing to do."

He considered her serene face, knowing it was a solution that never would have occurred to *him.*

But then it was becoming clearer with every passing day that he didn't understand her nearly as well as he'd once thought he did.

Her reaction to the Explorer was a case in point. He'd picked it out with her in mind, choosing the deep red paint and champagne leather interior as the perfect foil for her sunny beauty. But had she been excited by his surprise? Impressed by his thoughtfulness? Happy to have a new vehicle to drive?

Not so you'd notice. Oh, she'd been gracious enough, but in a restrained, I'd-prefer-you-hadn't-done-this sort of way. Which, he reminded himself, was better than her reaction when he'd bought her the parka. Initially she'd flatly refused to take it. He'd insisted, and they'd been locked in a stalemate until, out of sheer frustration, he'd suggested that if it made her feel better she could pay him back a little out of each paycheck. Clearly recognizing he was making a major concession, she'd agreed.

He had no intention of taking her money, of course. And though part of him had to admire her thorny pride, mostly he felt annoyed. She didn't seem to have any trouble spending his money when it came to Lissy. If he could afford nice things and wanted her to have them or, even more importantly, wanted to take care of a situation like the one with the mysterious Mr. Chapman, what was the problem?

He was damned if he knew. The only thing that was clear was that for someone he'd once considered a pampered princess, Eve was turning out to be a real challenge to spoil.

"John?"

"What?"

"Is everything all right?"

He glanced from her to Lissy, suddenly aware that both of them were staring curiously at him.

"Sure. I was just thinking about what needs to be done if we actually get the snow they're forecasting. Why?"

She smiled. "I've asked you twice already—would you care for some dessert? It's blueberry cobbler."

"Thanks, but I think I'll pass, at least for now."

"I want some!" Lissy was quick to assert.

Eve's smile widened. "Somehow, that doesn't surprise me." Climbing to her feet, she picked up their dishes and headed for the kitchen.

Eyes hooded, John watched her retreat. As if of its own volition, his gaze lingered on the elegant line of her back, noted the way her waist nipped in above her long, slender legs, recorded the feminine sway of her hips. Desire, always close to the surface where she was concerned, surged through him.

He tried to tell himself it was the sole cause of the ongoing frustration he felt but he knew it was a lie. Although it had only been a few weeks, he was fed up with having to constantly be discreet, sick of meeting resistance each time he tried to do something for Eve, annoyed that he didn't have more say in her life.

He'd worked hard to make a place for himself in the world where he was in charge, yet when it came to their relationship, none of that seemed to matter.

And he didn't like it. Even worse, he was damned if he knew what to do about it.

Eve took a firm grip on the ladder's side rail. Careful not to dislodge the plastic bottle of glass cleaner tucked under her arm, she leaned sideways with a wad of paper towels and scrubbed at the filmy streaks some enterprising bird had left on the outside of the great room's cathedral window.

Normally, washing windows was one of her least favorite tasks. But today it suited her mood. Although it was only a little after noon, the laundry was done, the house clean and in order, the pantry and freezer fully stocked since she'd shopped earlier in the week. She'd already started dinner, and it wasn't her day to be at school. She'd felt restless, in need of something physical to do, and hauling out the ladder, getting out in the fresh air and having a go at the windows fit the bill.

She just hadn't counted on it also leaving her plenty of time to think about John.

But then, lately he seemed to be on her mind most

of the time. Eve's mouth curved ruefully. She was starting to understand all the poems and songs dedicated to being in love, which she was finding tended to consume a person.

In her case, it was also making it increasingly difficult to stand by her principles and take things as they came, as she and John had agreed to do the first time they'd made love. She missed sleeping with him all night and waking up next to him in the morning. She wanted to feel free to seek him out, to claim him as hers in public, to spoil and fuss over him occasionally. Most of all, she wanted to tell him she loved him.

Except she was afraid of his reaction. There had been no compromise in his voice when he'd told her not to expect any long-term promises. All she could do was wait and hope that if she gave it enough time and didn't press, he'd change his mind and see how much he had to give. And he'd also see, she added a little grimly, glancing over at the gleaming Explorer peeking out of the parking shed, that she wanted him for him, and not for his money or because he could make her life easier.

A sudden gust of wind shook the ladder. Frowning, she decided she'd better finish while she still could and applied herself to the job with fresh vigor.

"What in the hell do you think you're doing?"

The unexpected sound of John's voice made her jump so she nearly lost her footing. Clutching the ladder, she swiveled around to find him standing below her, his hands on his narrow hips. "Good grief, you scared me." Despite her racing heart, she started to smile, happy to see him.

He glowered up at her. "You ought to be scared. Get down from there. Now."

Her smile vanished as she took in the steely expression that said he expected to be obeyed. Annoyed—he really was a slow study when it came to figuring out that she wouldn't put up with being ordered around—she said tartly, "Gee, John, it's nice to see you, too. I'll be down in a minute. I'm not quite done." With that, she resumed her task.

The next thing she knew, she felt the ladder flex and an arm like a steel band clamp around her middle. To her disbelief, a second after that she found herself tucked against John's side, being carried downward as if she weighed no more than a feather.

The minute her feet touched the ground, she wriggled free and turned to confront him. "What on earth do you think you're doing?"

He gave her a long, shuttered look and stooped to pick up his hat off the ground. "Getting you off that ladder before you break your neck."

"I'm perfectly capable of getting down under my own power if that's what I wanted—which I didn't."

"Tough. I'm not paying you to do this sort of labor."

She couldn't believe she'd heard him right. "What does that have to do with anything!"

"It has to do with the fact that you could've fallen through the damn window!"

Like a veil being torn away, she suddenly heard the anxiety beneath his anger. With dawning surprise, she realized she'd scared him, which opened the way for another, equally unexpected perception. "What are you doing here, anyway? I thought you had a meeting in Missoula."

"I canceled it."

"Why?"

He shrugged. "Because I felt like it."

"Why?" she persisted.

"Because." His voice held a telltale combination of belligerence and defensiveness. "The front they've been talking about all week finally seems to be moving in, and I didn't want to take a chance on leaving you and Lissy here alone, all right?"

The admission stripped away the last of her irritation and flooded her with tenderness. She could feel her face soften as she looked up at him. "All right." Her smile was back, tugging at the corners of her mouth. "And I'm sorry I scared you."

He scowled. "I wasn't scared. I just don't want you taking stupid risks."

"Right. I'll try to restrain myself in the future. After all, who needs clean windows? It's not as if we need to see out..."

He gave her a sour look. "You done?"

"Not if I can help it."

They considered each other. Later, she wasn't sure who took the first step, not that it mattered. John shook his head and murmured, "Damn, but you make me crazy," and then she was in his arms.

Eve drank him in, the knowledge that he cared warming her as much as the hot, drugging pressure of his lips. She sighed with pleasure as he cupped the side of her face with one big hand, lost in the contrast between his calloused palm and his gentle touch.

Everything around her faded away. She couldn't hear the breeze that made the fir trees creak overhead or feel the cold. Only John mattered, and by the time he took a deep, sustaining breath and lifted his head, she'd lost all sense of time. "No," she automatically protested as he took half a step back.

He looked down at her, and the skin at the edges of his eyes crinkled. "It's cold out here," he said with a rough edge to his voice. "Let's go inside."

"Yes."

He quickly pressed another brief kiss to her throbbing lips, then walked over, wrestled the ladder onto its side and propped it against the house. That task completed, he claimed her hand and headed for the porch. He didn't touch her anywhere else, but she could feel his tension, just as she could feel the need that now flowed wordlessly between them.

Once through the door, she started to reach for him but he shook his head. "No, not here," he said tersely. "Anybody could look in."

He twisted the lock. Boot heels ringing on the stone floor, he led her into the kitchen. The house felt warm after the frigid outside air and was filled with the delicious aroma of the stew she'd started that morning.

Neither of them paid any attention. Instead, they had eyes only for each other as John pressed her back against the nearest cabinet, winnowed his hands into her hair and kissed her again.

His hands and his face were cold, but his lips were warm. Eve groaned at the sweetness of it, wanting all of him that she could get. She slid her hands into his open coat and crowded closer. Tugging his shirt free of his jeans, she stroked the warm hollow at the small of his back and pressed her aching nipples against his hard chest.

He made a low sound deep in his throat. His mouth feasted on hers, making promises that made her temperature rise. He was so incredibly male, from the clean scent of his skin to the air of leashed power that was uniquely his. She skimmed her hands up his smooth, sleek back, glorying in the firm bulge of muscle beneath her palms. Need twisted through her, setting off an ache only he could satisfy.

He raised his head, breathing hard.

"John." She pressed her mouth to his throat.

Angling back, he unzipped her coat, unbuttoned her moss green flannel shirt and peeled both garments back. She opened her eyes and looked down, her pulse throbbing at the sight of his bronzed fingers against her paler skin. His hands were steady as he undid the center hook on her white lace bra and cupped her bare breasts in his palms.

He lowered his head and she gasped as he rubbed his cheek against her tender flesh a second before his mouth latched onto one distended nipple. The ache at her core grew as he suckled, drawing on that sensitized morsel, while his fingers shaped its mate. She forgot to breathe, her head falling back as his cool, dark hair tickled against her and his clever lips built on her need. "John," she whimpered. "Oh, please."

He released her, resting his head for a moment against the slope of her breast before he straightened. "I know, princess. I want you, too." His eyes gleaming like a slice of midnight, he worked at the snap of her jeans while she toed off her shoes. His fingers found the zipper, tugged, then gripped her waistband and slid the soft denim down. As her jeans hit the floor, he lifted her onto the counter.

Freeing himself from his own clothing, he wrapped an arm around her waist and guided himself inside her. She clutched his shoulders, unable to contain a moan as his body sank into hers, hard, hot and deep. "Yes. Like that." She gripped his shoulders tighter.

He tangled his hand in her hair and tugged, baring the long smooth line of her throat to his questing mouth. The slow slide of his lips made her shiver as he painted a trail of fire from her jaw to her collarbone. And all the while, they rocked together, slowly at first, and then faster and harder.

Eve wrapped her legs around him, unable to contain another soft cry as she realized she was on the verge of exploding. With a sudden sense of urgency, she cupped his chin in her hand and guided his mouth to hers, needing to kiss him, to try and tell him without words all that was in her heart.

And then, like a swimmer caught by an incoming wave, pleasure slammed into her, lifting her up, tossing her toward an exquisite shore. She felt herself tighten around John, felt the fullness as he pressed deep inside her, heard the cry he couldn't contain as her climax triggered his own. Mouth to mouth, heart to heart, they tumbled together on a crest of pleasure that seemed to go on forever.

It was long minutes later before Eve slowly surfaced. Feeling deliciously boneless, she lay nestled against John, her head on his shoulder, her body anchored by the muscular strength of his arms.

Slowly, she opened her eyes and a smile lit her face. "John?"

"Hmm?"

"Look." She raised her head and gestured to the window. "It's snowing."

Ten

    Snow swirled in the pickup's headlights, a curtain of white against a tar-black night.

John clenched his teeth and did his best to ignore his wet, clammy clothing. He concentrated instead on holding the pickup steady against the gusting wind and told himself to be grateful for small favors. Like the line of reflectors topping the fence posts that marched along both sides of the driveway.

Still, he couldn't deny he'd like to have ten minutes alone with the irresponsible fool who'd lost control of his car on the highway, taken out a portion of Bar M fence and then driven off without alerting anybody.

Thank God the ranch was as remote as it was. That most folks from these parts had better sense than to go out in a snowstorm. And that one of the few who didn't was Mitch, his foreman, who'd been on his way back from town when he'd come across a dozen head of Bar M cattle standing in the road.

As long as he was counting his blessings, John supposed he should also be glad that the beasts were now all safely corralled, the fence temporarily shored up, and it looked as if he was actually going to make it home before he succumbed to frostbite.

Home. Just the thought of it brought a kick of anticipation. He tried to shrug it off, only to abruptly sigh. It was no use kidding himself. For the first time in his life he actually had somebody—or rather, two somebodies—waiting for him. And try as he might to tell himself not to be foolish, it made him feel warm inside.

But then, he'd felt that way for the better part of the day, and not just because of what had happened once he'd gotten Eve off that damn ladder. As fiercely as he'd enjoyed their lovemaking, he'd also discovered he trusted her to manage during the storm, to take care of Lissy and do what needed to be done around the house, leaving him free to concentrate on making sure the ranch was in order.

It was a nice feeling, if a little strange. He'd never had anyone to rely on before. But then, there were a lot of things about his relationship with Eve that were new for him. Not the least of which was that lately he'd found himself thinking about her at odd moments in the day, wishing she were there to talk to, wondering what she'd say about one thing or another. If he didn't know better, he might actually think he was starting to depend on her.

It was an unsettling thought, and he shook it off as he peered through the windshield. Unfortunately, what he could see of the surrounding landscape looked like a foreign country thanks to the blowing snow. Instinct told him he should be close to the turnoff for the house, but he still would have missed it if not for a bobbing circle of light up ahead. Frowning, he eased the pickup to the left, and his headlights illuminated a slender figure hunched against the wind, waving a Coleman lantern.

Eve. He swore under his breath, his anticipation replaced by aggravation as he eased past her, turned into the yard and pulled into the dark garage. The sight of her outside in such treacherous weather made him feel a little crazy, the way he had earlier today when he'd caught her up on the ladder. Face grim, he climbed from the truck as she walked up, her slim figure buffeted by the wind.

"Hi." Ignoring his thunderous look, she stepped close and gave him a quick hug.

"What the blazes are you doing out here?" He had to raise his voice to make himself heard.

She retreated half a step. "The power's out. I was afraid you'd drive right past the house."

He sent her a look of disbelief. "So you were just going to stand out in the road until I showed up?"

"Of course not. Mitch called and said you were on your way, so Lissy and I've been watching for your headlights." She looked up at him, her gray eyes level despite the snowflakes frosting her thick lashes. "It's getting late. I was worried about you."

Her unexpected admission rekindled that warm feeling in his gut. Disconcerted, he took refuge in action and started herding her toward the porch. "I can take care of myself," he said gruffly.

"I know you can. But—" she broke off as they struggled up the stairs and he wrestled open the door

"—that doesn't change how I feel." The last words were said as they knocked the snow off their boots and jeans and hurried inside.

He grunted, still not knowing what to say, when a small figure emerged out of the semidarkness and hurled herself at him. "Are you okay, Daddy?"

He looked down to find Lissy clinging to the front of his jacket, gazing anxiously up at him. Apparently both the females in his life had a low opinion of his ability to take care of himself. It would have been humiliating if it weren't so damned endearing. "I'm fine, honey."

"He just needs to get warmed up." Eve set the lantern on the counter and stripped off her gloves, hat and coat. She laid her hand on his arm, only to recoil. "Your clothes are wet!"

"Yeah. I noticed."

"What happened?"

"Steer knocked me into the ditch." Though the house felt warm after the air outside, he couldn't entirely quell a shiver.

She sucked in her breath. "Good grief, John. You're lucky you don't have hypothermia. Lissy, why don't you get your dad a cup of the hot chocolate we made while he gets out of these clothes."

"Okay!"

The child darted out of the room before he could object, so he turned his frown on Eve, uncomfortable with being fussed over. "I don't need any hot chocolate," he protested. "And if I did, I could get it myself."

"Of course you could. But Lissy needs something to do. She's been worried about you, too."

There didn't seem to be anything he could say to

that, so he settled for unbuttoning his coat, only to find his hands were clumsy with cold.

"Here. Let me." She brushed his ineffective fingers away and had him stripped down to his long-john bottoms in no time.

He might be tired and half-frozen, but her touch had its usual effect on him. Need curled like a fist low in his belly, and only the thought of Lissy's imminent return gave him the strength to catch Eve by the wrist when she reached for his waistband. "I'd better take it from here."

Her gaze flew to his face, and whatever she saw there had her struggling not to smile. "Spoilsport," she murmured.

He tried to look stern but couldn't entirely hide the answering smile that tugged at his lips. "You're dangerous."

Lissy walked slowly back into the room, an oversize mug clutched carefully in both her small hands. "Here, Daddy."

He started to tell her he really didn't care for chocolate, only to fall silent at the expectant look on her face. With a sigh, he took the mug and raised it to his lips. To his surprise the rich, hot drink tasted wonderful. He drained the cup before he finally looked up. "Thanks. That was great."

Lissy beamed.

"Now why don't you two clear out and give me a second to change?"

Eve pulled off her boots and set them out of the way. "All right. There are dry clothes for you on top of the dryer."

"Okay." He reached over and snagged the navy thermal weave top she'd set out as she and Lissy headed into the other room. He pulled on the soft garment, trying to convince himself his sudden sense of contentment stemmed merely from being home, and not from Eve and Lissy's warm reception. Yet he found himself hurrying to finish dressing, and he knew damn well it wasn't merely because he was anxious to cozy up to the fire.

Once clothed, he picked up the lantern and headed for the other room, pausing just past the kitchen. In the time that he'd been gone Eve and Lissy had hauled out the sleeping bags, quilts and pillows and laid them out in front of the fireplace. A log burned hot and steady in the grate, while a trio of automatic lanterns augmented its soft, flickering light. With the snow swirling outside the big windows at the far end of the room, the atmosphere felt intimate and cozy.

"Come on, Daddy." Already ensconced in her sleeping bag, with Eve seated on her left, Lissy patted the space to her right. "I get to be in the middle. Eve said."

"She did, huh?" His gaze found Eve's, and to his amusement she gave a slight, apologetic shrug. Despite the unfortunate sleeping arrangements, he didn't hesitate, however. The truth was he still felt chilled to the bone, and the lure of the warmth from the fire, not to mention the company, was more than he could resist. He crossed the room and gingerly lowered himself onto the makeshift bed. Scooting back, he followed Eve's example, propping his back against the couch and stretching his legs out toward the hearth.

The second he was settled Lissy gave an enormous yawn and scooted closer to him. "Daddy?"

"Hmm?"

She rested her head against his chest. "Do you think we'll be able to go outside tomorrow?"

"I don't know. Why?"

"I want to make a snowman."

"You do, huh?" The scent of her came up at him, lemon shampoo, talcum powder and freshly laundered flannel. She felt incredibly small and vulnerable as she lay against him. Without thinking, he slid an arm around her.

"Yeah. I've never made one before."

"You haven't?"

"No." She yawned again. "Grandma always said the cold made her bones ache, so I had to stay inside."

"Well, you won't have to tomorrow."

"Really?"

"I promise."

"I love you, Daddy."

The words caught him totally unprepared. Everything inside him seemed to go still for a moment, and then from a distance he heard someone with his voice say quietly, "I love you, too, Lissy."

"I know." With a happy little sigh, she burrowed a little closer and without further ado drifted off to sleep.

He gazed down at her slack face, amazed by the whole exchange. For a moment he wondered if he'd simply imagined it, and then he felt the touch of Eve's hand on his arm. He looked up and her expression told him he hadn't. "You okay?" she asked softly.

"Sure."

"Good."

He was the first to look away, shifting his gaze back to Lissy. "You think she'll wake up if I move her?"

"I think you're safe."

Reassured, he twisted sideways, carefully cradling the child's limp upper body in his arms as he slid her deeper into her sleeping bag. Without so much as a murmur, she rolled onto her tummy, buried her head into her pillow and settled more deeply into sleep.

He started to straighten, only to still as Eve reached over and gently brushed his hair off his forehead. She smiled. "I'm glad you're home."

He caught her hand and pressed it to his cheek. "Yeah. Me, too." They leaned toward each other, careful not to disturb Lissy as they came together for long, lingering kiss.

Desire rose in him like an incoming tide. But tonight it was wrapped in a layer of contentment that gave the ache in his body a certain sweetness. Cupping Eve's face in his hand, he broke the seal of their lips to press kisses over her chin and cheeks, luxuriating in the satin warmth of her skin, the silkiness of her hair, her light, pleasing fragrance.

It was with a sigh of regret that he finally straightened. Neither of them spoke. As their gazes met, there didn't seem to be a need for words. Linking her fingers with his, he settled back and lay down on his makeshift bed, bunching the pillow under his head.

The heat from the fire settled over him like a blanket and his eyes grew heavy as the long day caught up with him. And yet he felt a sense of peace and belonging he'd never felt before.

His last thought as he drifted to sleep was that this must be how it felt to be a part of a family.

It was the quiet that woke John.

He stared blankly into the darkness. The only sounds in the room were the steady rhythm of Eve's and Lissy's breathing and the occasional pop of the log in the fireplace.

With a start, he realized the wind had stopped. Craning his head, he looked out the window to find that it was no longer snowing and that the sky beyond the glass was an expanse of navy-blue studded with stars. He glanced at the luminous dial on his watch. It was just coming up on four o'clock.

He rolled onto his back. Then, driven by a need he didn't question, he turned to consider Eve. She was lying on her side, her cheek resting on her arm, her lovely face serene. Her other arm was curved protectively over Lissy, who was cuddled against her.

Watching her, he felt an unfamiliar swell of emotion. He might not love her, he realized, but he cared. More than he'd ever cared for a woman. More than he'd ever cared for anyone except for his daughter. In addition, he liked her. He liked her independence and her wry sense of humor, her courage, her integrity and her obvious femininity. He also knew that she was good for him, bringing a balance to his life he'd only recently begun to understand that he needed.

If he had any sense at all, he'd marry her.

The instant the thought registered, he dismissed it. Yet as he continued to lay there, his gaze on Eve's face, the idea persisted, refusing to go away.

Why *not* marry her? he asked himself slowly.

He knew she loved Lissy. He also thought her feelings for him ran deep. And not only were they extremely sexually compatible but he was genuinely fond of her.

A union between them would benefit everybody. Lissy would get a mother she adored. He'd get the security of knowing his home and his daughter were in good hands, as well as the freedom to indulge this compulsion he had to take care of her. As for Eve, once again she'd have someone to provide for her the way her grandfather had. She'd be able to buy pretty clothes, drive a nice car, do all the things she couldn't afford on her salary as his nanny.

There were worse things on which to base a marriage.

Not that he expected it to last, not forever. Eventually, inevitably, she'd leave. But by the time she did, he'd be ready. The sexual fire that blazed between them now would no doubt have burned down, if not flamed out. This inexplicable need he had to be with her, to touch her and talk to her and protect her, would have faded away. And Lissy would be older....

In the meantime, however, the benefits clearly outweighed the drawbacks.

Still, he continued to debate with himself, weighing the pros and cons, going over it again and again.

Eventually, however, the decision was made. And when it was, a profound sense of peace settled over him and all the frustration he'd felt recently seemed to drain away. Settling his head more deeply into the pillow, he knew as he finally fell back asleep that he was doing the right thing.

The morning sunshine sparkled on the snow that stretched as a vast white blanket in every direction.

Ignoring the slight ache in her lungs from breathing the frigid air, Eve narrowed her eyes against the dazzling light and watched as John lifted Lissy up so she could put her snowman's head in place. Once the oversize ball was securely situated, he set the child on her feet and took a step back to consider their creation. "What do you think?"

Lissy considered, her small face grave. "It's perfect," she said solemnly. "Only…"

"What?"

"It doesn't got a face."

"Good point."

Eve smiled. "I think I can help with that."

Lissy turned eagerly toward her. "You can?"

"Uh-huh." She dug into her coat pockets and pulled out the items she'd gathered before venturing outside. "I thought these would work for eyes—" she handed the child a plastic bag holding a pair of Oreo cookies "—and I brought a carrot for the nose and—" She held up another bag, "I thought we could use chocolate chips for the mouth."

"Perfect," Lissy crowed. "But what about the buttons for his coat?"

"I thought we could use gravel from the drive." She smiled sweetly at John. "Your father can get it."

"Thanks a lot." His attempt to look forbidding failed miserably, given the way his blue eyes gleamed with good humor.

But then, he'd been in a good mood all morning, Eve thought, as she watched him stride over to the driveway and begin digging through the snow. From the moment Lissy had shook them awake to excitedly inform them the sun was shining, he'd seemed uncharacteristically lighthearted. And though she couldn't help but wonder at the source, she also couldn't deny that it made him seem younger and even more wildly attractive.

Lissy tugged on her coat. "Will you lift me up, Eve, so I can do the face?"

"Sure." Tearing her gaze away from John, she did just that, and by the time he rejoined them, they were almost done.

Not that he seemed impressed with their progress. Frowning slightly, he reached over and plucked Lissy out of her arms and into his. "You shouldn't be lifting her. She's too heavy," he said as the child put the last chocolate chip into place.

"I'm stronger than I look," she replied demurely.

He didn't comment, just set Lissy on the ground and handed her the rocks he'd collected. Both of them watched as she promptly used them to decorate the snowman's midsection.

"Are you happy now?" He asked his daughter when she was done.

She nodded. "Except..."

"Now what?"

"He looks sort of...naked."

John raised his eyes to heaven. "Well, yeah. He's a snowman."

"I know. But he ought to have on something."

"You're right." Smothering a smile, Eve unwound her muffler and wrapped it around the snowman's neck. "There. How's that?"

Lissy bit her lip. "But won't you get cold?"

Before she could answer, John surprised them both by removing his hat and plopping it on Eve's head. "Not as long as I'm around. That'll help. So will this."

Without warning, he reached out, caught her in his arms and kissed her soundly.

"Daddy!" Lissy let loose with a shriek that was half protest and half excited little girl giggle.

With an exaggerated air of reluctance, he broke off

the kiss and looked down at his daughter, eyebrows raised. "What?"

"You kissed Eve!"

His mouth twitched. "Yeah, I know."

"But how come?"

"Because I like her."

"You do?"

"Yeah. Don't you?"

"Of course!"

Without further ado, he reached over and pulled the child close, so she was cuddled between them. "That's because you're a MacLaren." He looked down, gave her small body a gentle squeeze, then looked straight back at Eve and grinned. "And we MacLarens have exceptionally good taste."

Eve looked at his incredibly handsome face, her heart melting, as for the first time ever, she saw the deep groove—in anyone less masculine she would have termed it a dimple—that bracketed the left side of his mouth. "I'm not going to argue with that," she murmured, smiling back. And because she couldn't help herself, she wrapped her hand around the back of his head, leaned forward and kissed him again.

The feel of his warm lips in the cold air was delicious. What's more, there was a kind of tender possessiveness in his touch today that made her stomach hollow and her breath hitch. Leaning into him, she lost all track of time as the world seemed to narrow to the taste of his mouth, the grip of his hand, the slippery softness of his hair beneath her fingertips.

"Gosh." Lissy's voice held a note of awe. "Don't you guys need to breathe or something?"

John's mouth curved against hers, and then he pulled back and chuckled. In all the time she'd known him, it was the first time Eve had ever heard him really laugh, and the sound seemed to fill her like champagne, making her dizzy.

Looking into his laughing face, she was overcome by her feelings for him.

She loved him. And it was past time that she told him.

Eleven

Eve shut the Explorer's door and started up the walkway to the house.

Although the temperature was only in the high thirties, most of the weekend's snowfall was gone, thanks to three days of weak but steady sunshine. The one exception was Lissy's snowman, which continued to grace the yard with its cheerful, if now decidedly lopsided, presence.

Careful to watch for icy patches, Eve pattered up the porch steps. Juggling her purse, a bag of groceries and a stack of mail, she opened the door and stepped inside. She proceeded into the kitchen, set down her burdens, shrugged out of her coat, then put it and her purse away. Next she unloaded the groceries, checked on the chicken she'd put in the oven earlier and, on a whim, started a fire in the fireplace.

Finally out of obvious things to do, she slowly approached the kitchen counter, carefully stacked John's mail next to the telephone and reluctantly considered the large manila envelope she'd picked up from Gus Bolt's office earlier in the day. The return address label left no doubt as to who sent the package—Morris Chapman's name was there in bold printing, as was the listing of a post office box in Two Pennies, New Mexico.

Eve sighed. The past few days had been magical. Not only had John's good mood persisted but he seemed finally to be at ease with Lissy, and the improvement in their relationship had been dramatic. And even though the world seemed to be conspiring to make sure she and John never got a moment alone, Eve didn't mind.

It didn't seem right that reality had to choose now to intrude. But then, hadn't she learned by now that life wasn't always fair? And that bad things didn't go away, no matter how long one procrastinated?

Squaring her shoulders, she picked up the envelope, walked over to the table and sat. Taking a calming breath, she tore the flap and pulled out a sheaf of papers.

She loosened the clip holding them all together. On top was a letter. She set it aside and thumbed through what appeared to be a mining company prospectus, only to dislodge a rectangle of pale green paper.

It fluttered to the tabletop, and she stared at it in amazement. It was a check, issued by the Two Pennies Mine. And it was made out to her, in the amount of sixty-five thousand dollars.

For a moment she couldn't breathe, could only stare.

Finally, however, the worst of her shock passed. With an almost steady hand, she picked up the letter, which proved to be short and to the point.

According to Mr. Chapman, her grandfather had invested in his struggling silver mine seven years ago. After nearly a decade of barely breaking even, the mine had hit pay dirt nine months ago, when a huge vein of silver had been discovered. The enclosed check was the first return on Max's money. Mr. Chapman sent his assurances that there would be more to follow.

Eve sat motionless, the words blurring on the page as she tried to take it in. After all her worry, it appeared she didn't owe Mr. Chapman money after all. On the contrary, she'd come into a windfall, with the promise of more to come.

She shook her head, as if to clear it, and considered what this would have meant to her a few months ago.

She never would have come begging to John for a job. She would have left Lander without ever coming to know—or love—him and Lissy.

Just the idea made her shudder.

And now? she asked herself.

Now it didn't matter. She was where she wanted to be, with the two people she loved most in the world. The only difference was that now she'd have some added security. And—she couldn't contain a smile— she'd be able to indulge herself. Come Christmas, not only would she be able to afford the super-deluxe Barbie house Lissy had seen in the Sears catalog but she'd also be able to get John the exquisitely beautiful saddle she'd seen the last time she'd been to Missoula.

Just the thought made her smile.

Her head came up as she heard the back door open and close, followed by the familiar sound of John's footsteps. Without thinking, she gathered the check, the letter and the rest of the papers, turned them over and stacked them on top of the envelope. She'd tell him about her good news, but later, after she'd had more time to absorb it herself.

There was something far more important she wanted to tell him first, if only she could find the right time.

"Hey," he said, looking big and vital as he strode into the room.

"Hey yourself." Unable to help herself, she climbed to her feet, closed the distance between them and went up on tiptoe to give him a welcoming kiss. For a second he stiffened, and then his arms came around her and the pressure of his mouth increased. She couldn't contain a soft sound of pleasure at the solid strength of his chest against hers and the muscular press of his arms.

It was awhile before they separated.

When they did, John took an audible breath and leaned his forehead against hers. "That was nice. Where's Lis?"

"Having dinner at Jenny's. I told Lois I'd pick her up around eight."

A gleam ignited in his eyes at the breathlessness in her voice. "In that case…"

To her consternation, he put her away from him and headed purposefully for the mudroom. Gathering her scattered wits, she was about to ask what he was doing when he reappeared, a sleeping bag tucked under his arm.

She watched as he unzipped the thick bedroll and spread it out before the fire. Leaning against the back of one of the club chairs, he yanked off his boots, set them out of the way and straightened, his hands going to his shirt buttons. His gaze played over her, his eyes looking very blue in the light as a lazy smile transformed his handsome face. "I've been thinking about making love to you in front of the fire ever since Friday night," he informed her.

His smile, still so new, made her knees feel ridiculously weak. "In that case, I suppose it's all right to admit that so have I." Her gaze never leaving his, she began stripping her own clothes away.

"You have?"

"Absolutely."

He made no effort to hide his satisfaction at her answer. Tall and straight, his wide shoulders, washboard stomach, narrow hips and long lean thighs outlined by the fire as dusk filled the room, he simply waited.

Naked, she stepped toward him.

He looked at her one endless moment. "You're so damn beautiful, Eve." He slid his hands into her hair, holding her still as he lowered his head. "Say my name," he whispered. "I need to hear you say my name."

"John." She slid her hands over his satiny shoulders and gazed steadily at him. "John."

With a groan, his mouth settled over hers, hot and sweet. Her pulse leaped. An insistent ache bloomed between her thighs as the kiss went on and on, their only point of contact, until finally he wrapped an arm around her waist and carried her down to the sleeping bag.

Never relinquishing her mouth, his hands found hers and he twined their fingers together as he stretched her arms above her head. "Sweet," he murmured fiercely. And then, as his body rocked, sliding home between her open thighs, he whispered, "I need you. Damn it, I need you too much."

With a sob, she arched beneath him, the unexpected words igniting her blood with fire. In that instant the love she felt for him was overwhelming, and despite the suddenness of his possession, she was more than ready, her body already trembling on the verge of release.

Sensation flooded her as he surged into her, thick and hot. She couldn't get enough. Not of the strong grip of his hands holding hers, the way his back hollowed as she wrapped her legs around his waist, the delicious pressure of his chest rubbing against her sensitized nipples. Not of the feel of him as he drove into her over and over, and heat seemed to scorch her from the inside out.

She strained against him, crying out. "Yes. John. Yes...." She struggled for the absolute pleasure that beckoned tantalizingly just out of reach, wanting that completion even as she longed for their union to go on. "I love you." She couldn't hold back the words any longer, any more than she could stop the feelings that ran so deep inside her. "I love you so much."

For a second he went still, and then he shuddered as the last of his control vanished. Sobbing for breath, his hips driving like a piston, he thrust full into her, crying out as she clamped down around him and his whole body tensed with his climax, triggering her own. Wave after wave of pleasure poured through her.

Holding tight to each other, they clung together for so long that Eve lost track of time. All she knew was that she'd never felt this way about anyone before in her life, as if they were one body, one breath, one heartbeat.

John raised his head minutes later. Carefully shifting his weight onto his elbows, he looked down at her. "You all right?"

A languorous smile tugged at her mouth. "Uh-huh."

To her dismay, she could have sworn there was a shadow in his eyes that hadn't been there before. There was no hint of it in his voice, however. "Good. That's good," he said as he rolled onto his back, keeping her close.

Telling herself she must have imagined it, she nestled closer and waited for her heart to quit pounding, savoring the feel of him against her, all warm and densely muscled.

Outside, the sky had darkened to charcoal as day slipped inexorably into night. Inside, the fire had burned down to a steady wave of flame that bathed the room in a rosy light. As the minutes passed, she relaxed. Pillowing her head on his arm, she sighed with contentment as she pressed a kiss to the bend of his elbow. Slowly, her breathing evened out. Her eyelids grew heavy, and she decided it couldn't possibly hurt to close them just for a moment.

When Eve awoke, the room was dark and John was sitting beside her, his back propped against the couch.

At some point he'd pulled on his jeans and covered her with a blanket. Warmed by his thoughtfulness—not to mention the compelling picture he made as he stared into the fire—she lightly touched her hand to his bare chest. "Hi."

He looked down at her, and there was a look in his eyes she'd never seen before. "Welcome back."

"How long was I out?"

"About an hour."

"What?" Clutching the blanket to her breasts, she sat up. "Dinner must be a cinder."

"Relax." He stroked his hand down her exposed spine. "I turned down the oven a while ago."

"Oh." She settled back next to him. "Well, thanks."

He shrugged, watching as a piece of the log in the fireplace gave way and sent up a shower of sparks. The silence stretched for several seconds before he shifted and gave her a long, searching look. "Did you mean it when you said you loved me?" he asked abruptly.

Somehow she'd known the question was coming. "Yes. Of course I did."

Some of the tension left his face. "I think we ought to get married."

She was so stunned that for a moment she forgot to breathe. She wasn't sure what she'd expected, but it wasn't this. "You do?"

"Yeah. I know we haven't been together that long, but as much as I like these stolen moments—" he took a pointed look around at their temporary nest "—they're not enough. I want people to know you're mine. Just like I want the right to take you to my bed at night and wake up beside you the next morning.''

Her heart squeezed. Until this very moment, she'd had no idea how much she wanted to be his wife. But she did. She wanted to spend the rest of her life with him, have his children, be the one he turned to with his hopes and dreams, his disappointments and his triumphs.

Misreading her silence, he went on persuasively, ''Think about it, Eve. You'd get a nice home. A kid who's crazy about you. And you wouldn't have to worry about money. I can give you everything that Max did and more, so you'll be able to have the sort of luxuries you did before. Except for the travel, you'll have your old life back.''

With every word, the warm glow she'd felt just seconds earlier dissipated. ''Is that what you think I want?'' she asked slowly.

''I suppose I could dress it up in prettier words, but yeah—why not? You're a beautiful woman. You deserve nice things. And why would anyone bother to get married if it wasn't to their benefit?''

''I see. And in this case, you get sex and I get money?'' Her voice sounded remarkably calm. Which was a surprise, given that she felt as if her heart were breaking. Suddenly chilled, she looked around but her bra and panties were nowhere to be found, so she simply pulled on her sweater and jeans without them. ''I believe there's a name for that, John. And it's definitely *not* 'marriage.''' She stood and stepped into her shoes.

He climbed to his feet as well. ''Damn it, Eve, don't twist what I'm saying! It's not that I don't have feelings for you. I do. But if you're waiting for some big romantic declaration, you'd better accept that it's not going to happen.''

Ignoring the hurt his words brought her, she raised her chin in challenge. ''And why is that?''

''Because it's not who I am. I gave up on all that happily ever after stuff as a kid. There's nothing like growing up the way I did to teach you that the whole love thing is highly overrated. From what I've seen, it doesn't last. Give me a well-crafted business deal any day.''

She stared into his stony face, appalled to realize he believed what he was saying. Rubbing her arms, she paced across the room, not turning until she reached the table. ''But how can you say that? Look what's happened with you and Lissy. I know you love her—''

''That's different,'' he said sharply, stalking toward her.

''Maybe it is. But you had no way of knowing it was going to be. So why did you ever agree to take her in the first place?''

''Why the hell do you think? She's my flesh and blood. There was no way I was going to turn my back on her, not after—'' He abruptly caught himself and broke off, the familiar shuttered look appearing on his face.

''Not after what?'' she persisted.

''It doesn't matter.''

She didn't believe him, not for an instant. She replayed his words and out of nowhere found herself completing his sentence in a way that made what was happening between them fall into place. ''You couldn't turn your back on Lissy the way your mother did on you," she said slowly. "Isn't that what you were going to say?"

"I told you it doesn't matter."

"I think it does." Her mind continued to work, and she decided to take a chance. "Do you remember the morning the horse got loose?"

He looked at her woodenly. "What about it?"

"When I got up, I was cold, so I decided to borrow one of the T-shirts out of your dresser. I didn't mean to pry, but I found the jacket and the note your mother left you."

"You had no damn right—"

She ignored him. "At the time, I thought you'd kept those things because they were all you had to connect you with her, but now...I wonder..."

"You wonder what?" His voice was colder than a mountain creek in the dead of winter.

"I wonder if you kept them to remind you that people who claim to love you can't be trusted, that they'll hurt you in the end."

"You don't know what the hell you're talking about." His movements stiff with undisguised anger, he started to turn away, and his thigh bumped the table, sending the papers from Morris Chapman fluttering to the floor. Swearing, he stooped down to gather them up, only to suddenly stiffen as his gaze zeroed in on the check. He picked it up and gave it a long look, and as he did, a veil seemed to come down over his eyes.

Straightening, he tossed the check and the rest of the papers onto the table. "So much for true love," he said scornfully. "No wonder you're not interested in marrying me."

"What?"

"Apparently you've come into some money. At least you could have told me the truth instead of putting us both through this farce—"

"You're a fool if you believe that," she said flatly.

"Am I?"

"Yes. I love you, John. And no matter what you say or how badly you behave, that's not going to change."

"Yeah, right."

His sensual, arrogant mouth compressed into a mulish line.

She walked over and picked up her keys and purse. "I'm going to get Lissy now. But when I get back..." She considered his hard, closed expression and suddenly feared that no matter what she said, he wasn't going to listen.

Still, she had to try, even if it meant trying to shock him into reason. "When I get back, I'll pack my things and go." Holding her breath as she waited for his reaction, she headed for the door.

He didn't say a word.

"Daddy?"

John looked up from his computer screen to find Lissy standing just inside the study doorway.

He'd heard her and Eve come into the house more than an hour ago but had deliberately opted to stay in his office. For one thing, he had a ton of paperwork to catch up on since lately—due to certain distractions—he'd let things slide. More to the point, what could possibly be gained by another confrontation? He and Eve had said more than enough. And he was damned if he'd expose Lissy to something he felt strongly shouldn't concern her.

Except it was obvious from the child's stricken expression that Eve hadn't shown the same discretion. With a mixture of anger and dismay, he considered his daughter, noting the eyes jeweled with tears and the ominously trembling lower lip. Despite her cheerful outfit of pink flannel pajamas and bunny slippers, she looked as if she'd just lost her very best friend.

Or learned she was about to. "What is it, Lissy?"

She hesitated for the briefest instant, then dashed across the thickly padded rug and flung herself into his arms. "Eve's leaving," she cried, dissolving into tears.

So. She was really going through with it.

A heavy weight seemed to press against his chest. Stubbornly, he shook off the sensation, telling himself that what he was feeling was merely concern for Lissy. He patted her small, shaking back and tried to find the words to reassure her. "I know she is. But you don't need to worry about it. We'll be fine without her, baby, I promise."

She raised her tear-streaked face to his. "But I d-don't want to be without her!" Swallowing hard, she took a long shuddering breath, struggling for control over the sobs still threatening to overwhelm her. "She says she'll see me at school and she'll come to my dance recital, but it w-won't be the same." Her voice rose. "Can't you make her stay?"

The old, familiar frustration at not knowing the right thing to say swept him. "Lissy…"

"Please, Daddy?" Tucked against his shoulder, she

looked up at him imploringly, her blue eyes huge in her small face.

For an instant he wavered, wishing he could grant her her desire. But then an image of Eve walking out the door flashed through his mind, and he felt a fresh rush of anger. After all, his only crime was that he'd offered her a mutually advantageous marriage, and what had she done? She'd thrown it back in his face, making it clear that what he had to offer wasn't good enough.

Which only proved what he'd known all along: when push came to shove, love wasn't worth much. His face hardened. "I can't, Lis."

"But why not? Did—did you guys have a fight?"

He regarded her earnest little face and realized that this, at least, was a reason she could understand. What's more, in its simplest sense, it was true. "Yeah. You could say that."

"Oh." Biting her lip, she contemplated her slippers and appeared to consider his answer. After a moment she let out a shuddery breath and said in a small, uncertain voice, "If we have a fight, will I have to go away?"

Aw, hell. "No. *No.*" He tightened his arms around her. "Nothing you could do would ever make me send you away," he said forcefully. "You're my kid, and you're here to stay. Okay?"

She looked up, relief mixed with consternation on her face. "But I know Eve loves you. She said so. She said you and me mattered most to her in the world. And you're making *her* go away."

"No, I'm not. She made the choice—"

"But you won't even try to make her stay," she insisted with perfect, seven-year-old logic.

He searched for patience. "Look, you remember how I told you I grew up in an orphanage?"

She nodded solemnly. "Uh-huh."

"Well, it taught me some things. And one is that you can't always trust what people say."

Her brow puckered. "You mean they lie?"

He frowned. Somehow it didn't sound quite the way he'd intended said straight out like that. "Well, yeah."

"But why would Eve do that?"

He gazed down at his daughter, into those eyes that were the exact same blue as his own, and abruptly realized he didn't have an answer.

Two days ago—hell, two hours ago—he would have said Eve was just deluding herself, claiming she loved him because it was easier than admitting she wanted the security he could give her.

But that explanation didn't hold up very well in light of her newly acquired sixty-five thousand dollars.

Still, there had to be some logical reason, he assured himself. He was just too damn fed up with the whole subject to think of it at the moment. "I don't know," he said brusquely. "What I do know is what I learned when I was even younger than you are now. And that's that you can't depend on anyone but yourself."

The crease between Lissy's eyebrows deepened. "But that was a long time ago, Daddy." She worried her lower lip. "You're a grown-up now. And I depend on *you*. Or aren't I s'posed to?"

It was such a simple question, yet it pierced him to the core. Meeting his child's worried gaze, he felt the foundation he'd built his world on crumble as he gave her the only answer possible. "Well, sure. Of course you are."

She relaxed and nestled against him. "Good."

He barely heard her for the roaring in his head. Hell. He *was* a grown-up, he thought dazedly. The only problem was, he suddenly knew that on one particular subject he hadn't been thinking like one for a long, long time.

Eve had been right. She just hadn't taken it far enough. He *had* kept the note and the coat as a reminder of his mother's abandonment. Just as he'd taken what he'd seen in the orphanage and used it as proof that love, no matter how well-meaning, couldn't be counted on.

As a consequence, he'd spent his entire adult life avoiding emotional entanglements. But it wasn't because he didn't believe in love, he realized now.

It was because he did, since he'd seen its power and known firsthand what a toll its loss could take. Not to put too fine a point on it, but he'd been afraid.

And then Eve had shown up. And though he'd known she was a threat to his indifference right from the beginning, he'd been unable to resist her. But still he'd tried, throwing up every sort of barrier.

Now, however, he could see her clearly. And, among other things, he knew that when it came to money, she really didn't care. He was the one who'd put such a priority on it, because taking care of her had been his excuse for getting close while maintaining his emotional inaccessibility. All along he'd been secretly afraid that if she didn't have to depend on him financially, she'd leave him the way his mother had.

And in the end he'd managed to drive her away anyway.

"Daddy? Are you okay? You look funny."

He cleared his throat. "I'm fine, honey. I just…I do want Eve to stay. But I think I hurt her feelings and I don't know if I can make it right."

She patted his shoulder. "It's okay, Daddy. No matter what, Eve will forgive you."

He wasn't so sure, but as he stood to carry her into bed, he prayed she was right.

That's the last of it, Eve thought without the slightest trace of satisfaction, as she placed the last stack of her underthings into the largest of the two suitcases open on her bed. But then, it was hard to get too excited about being an efficient packer when you were preparing to leave a place—and the people— you'd come to love.

She squeezed her eyes shut, wondering yet again what had possessed her to push things with John the way she had. She should have been more diplomatic. She should have heard him out and told him she needed time to think about his proposal.

She should have done anything but what she had, rejecting his offer, calling him a fool, telling him she'd leave while praying he'd call her bluff. He was a proud man, and she'd painted him into a corner. If only she'd pretended to go along, she might have been able to talk to him later when they were both calmer—

Right. And at what cost? Or don't you remember what happened with Granddad when you chose to just "go along"?

She let loose a sigh and reluctantly faced the idea

that she'd done the only thing that she could. It had taken John more than thirty years to get where he was, and it was foolish of her to believe that anything she could say—today, tomorrow or a year from now— would make a difference. She knew better than anyone that change had to come from inside. It couldn't be dictated, or wished into existence.

For that reason alone, it was kinder by far to accept things the way they were and to let everyone involved get on with their lives. Even if she did feel as if her heart was breaking…

A faint sound came from the hallway. With a sixth sense that she didn't question, she knew it was John even before a quick glance at the doorway confirmed it. She looked away, wondering what he wanted, and praying that whatever it was, she could get through the encounter with her dignity intact.

She waited for him to say something. When he didn't, she flipped the larger suitcase shut, doing her best to appear calm. "There. That's everything, except for Lissy's pictures." She gestured in the general direction of the stack of drawings on her dresser. "I thought I'd put them in a paper bag and carry them so they won't get wrinkled." When he remained silent, she found herself chattering on. "Chrissy's coming to get me." She glanced at her watch, then closed and zipped the second suitcase. "She should be here within the hour. Is Lissy in bed?"

He spoke at last. "Yeah. I tucked her in a few minutes ago."

"Oh. I'll just go give her a good-night kiss then." Bracing herself, she turned. Unfortunately for her peace of mind, nothing had changed in the past few hours; he looked as tall, rugged and uncompromisingly male as ever, and she suddenly understood what it meant to love someone so much it hurt.

"I'd appreciate it if you'd hold off a minute." To her surprise, he shifted his weight onto his heels and shoved his hands into his back pockets in a way that, if he were any other man, would have made her think he was nervous.

Which was ridiculous. She'd seen John in all sorts of situations, and not once had he ever lacked for confidence. "I really don't think—"

"Please, Eve. Just listen."

Everything inside her protested; she didn't think she could bear to hear him tell her again that he'd never love her. On the other hand, he showed no intention of leaving, so short of trying to wrestle him out of the doorway it appeared she had no choice but to listen. "Okay."

"I want a second chance."

Her heart gave a painful lurch. "You do?"

"Yeah." He cleared his throat. "You were right about that stuff from my mother. I did keep it to remind me of the way she'd left me, and that love couldn't be trusted. I told myself I was just being honest, facing a truth that other people didn't have the guts to." A touch of irony colored his voice. "I didn't think of it as protecting myself. I just thought I was being independent.

"Then you showed up. And no matter how hard I fought it, I wanted you. Physically at first, it's true, but it didn't take long before I wanted more. Except that I was damned if I'd admit I was falling in love with you, because as long as I denied it, I thought I couldn't get hurt.'' His mouth twisted in a parody of a smile. ''Only it doesn't work that way—I know that now. Because no matter what I call it, being without you would be like being without the best part of myself.''

She blinked back the tears that were suddenly threatening to overflow. She wanted to stop him, to tell him he didn't need to go on, that she'd meant it when she said there was nothing he could do that would make her stop loving him. But she forced herself to remain silent, instinctively knowing he needed to get this out, no matter how difficult it was.

''I love you, Eve. I think I've loved you from the first time I saw you and I know I want us to spend the rest of our lives together. I'm not promising it'll be perfect. I'm not an easy man to live with, and I've been on my own for so long that I'm not very good at sharing my thoughts or my feelings. But if you'll stay, and give me a chance, I swear I'll do my best. Say you'll marry me, sweetheart. Please.''

''Yes. Oh, John, yes.'' Unable to wait a second longer, needing to touch him, she started forward, but before she could take more than a step he was moving toward her. He pulled her into his arms, and the feel of him was like heaven.

For a moment they just stood, holding each other. Eve could hear his heart pounding, and the physical evidence of his vulnerability only heightened the aching tenderness she already felt. ''I love you,'' she said quietly.

His arms tightened around her. ''Say it again.''

She smiled. ''I love you.''

He let out his breath. ''Thank God. I love you, too.''

Again, they were silent, savoring their closeness. It was minutes later before either of them spoke.

"I suppose I'd better call Chrissy." Eve rubbed her cheek against the smooth cotton covering John's chest, glorying in his warmth and strength.

His grip on her didn't change. "Good idea."

"And we probably ought to go talk to Lissy."

"Yeah. Probably." He stayed right where he was. "But first I'm going to kiss you. Maybe more than once."

She leaned back so she could see his face. His blue eyes blazed as he looked down at her, all of the emotion he'd suppressed for so long plainly visible for her to see.

She smiled. "That sounds like a good idea."

And it was.

* * * * *

*Look for RITA Award-winning author
Caroline Cross's next novel,
HUSBAND—OR ENEMY?
part of Desire's*

FORTUNE'S CHILDREN: THE GROOMS,

on sale November 2000

Silhouette® Desire

Proudly presents

Blood Brothers
(SD #1307)

Two great love stories... One super read... by top authors

Anne McAllister
and Lucy Gordon

Double trouble! That's what you get when Montana cowboy Gabe McBride and his cousin British lord Randall Stanton trade places. What Gabe and Randall got was the challenge of their lives as they attempted to woo two unforgettable women—with their British pluck and cowboy try!

Don't miss this irresistible romance... available July 2000 at your favorite retail outlet.

Silhouette®
Where love comes alive™

Multi-*New York Times* bestselling author

NORA ROBERTS

knew from the first how to capture readers' hearts.
Celebrate the 20th Anniversary of Silhouette Books
with this special 2-in-1 edition containing her fabulous
first book and the sensational sequel.

Coming in June

IRISH HEARTS

Adelia Cunnane's fiery temper sets proud, powerful horse
breeder Travis Grant's heart aflame and he resolves to
make this wild *Irish Thoroughbred* his own.

Erin McKinnon accepts wealthy Burke Logan's loveless
proposal, but can this ravishing *Irish Rose* win her
hard-hearted husband's love?

Also available in June from
Silhouette Special Edition (SSE #1328)

IRISH REBEL

In this brand-new sequel to *Irish Thoroughbred*, Travis and
Adelia's innocent but strong-willed daughter Keeley discovers
love in the arms of a charming Irish rogue with a talent for
horses...and romance.

Silhouette®
Where love comes alive™

SILHOUETTE'S 20TH ANNIVERSARY CONTEST
OFFICIAL RULES
NO PURCHASE NECESSARY TO ENTER

1. To enter, follow directions published in the offer to which you are responding. Contest begins 1/1/00 and ends on 8/24/00 (the "Promotion Period"). Method of entry may vary. Mailed entries must be postmarked by 8/24/00, and received by 8/31/00.

2. During the Promotion Period, the Contest may be presented via the Internet. Entry via the Internet may be restricted to residents of certain geographic areas that are disclosed on the Web site. To enter via the Internet, if you are a resident of a geographic area in which Internet entry is permissible, follow the directions displayed on-line, including typing your essay of 100 words or fewer telling us "Where In The World Your Love Will Come Alive." On-line entries must be received by 11:59 p.m. Eastern Standard time on 8/24/00. Limit one e-mail entry per person, household and e-mail address per day, per presentation. If you are a resident of a geographic area in which entry via the Internet is permissible, you may, in lieu of submitting an entry on-line, enter by mail, by hand-printing your name, address, telephone number and contest number/name on an 8"x 11" plain piece of paper and telling us in 100 words or fewer "Where In The World Your Love Will Come Alive," and mailing via first-class mail to: Silhouette 20th Anniversary Contest, (in the U.S.) P.O. Box 9069, Buffalo, NY 14269-9069; (In Canada) P.O. Box 637, Fort Erie, Ontario, Canada L2A 5X3. Limit one 8"x 11" mailed entry per person, household and e-mail address per day. On-line and/or 8"x 11" mailed entries received from persons residing in geographic areas in which Internet entry is not permissible will be disqualified. No liability is assumed for lost, late, incomplete, inaccurate, nondelivered or misdirected mail, or misdirected e-mail, for technical, hardware or software failures of any kind, lost or unavailable network connection, or failed, incomplete, garbled or delayed computer transmission or any human error which may occur in the receipt or processing of the entries in the contest.

3. Essays will be judged by a panel of members of the Silhouette editorial and marketing staff based on the following criteria:

   Sincerity (believability, credibility)—50%

   Originality (freshness, creativity)—30%

   Aptness (appropriateness to contest ideas)—20%

   Purchase or acceptance of a product offer does not improve your chances of winning. In the event of a tie, duplicate prizes will be awarded.

4. All entries become the property of Harlequin Enterprises Ltd., and will not be returned. Winner will be determined no later than 10/31/00 and will be notified by mail. Grand Prize winner will be required to sign and return Affidavit of Eligibility within 15 days of receipt of notification. Noncompliance within the time period may result in disqualification and an alternative winner may be selected. All municipal, provincial, federal, state and local laws and regulations apply. Contest open only to residents of the U.S. and Canada who are 18 years of age or older, and is void wherever prohibited by law. Internet entry is restricted solely to residents of those geographical areas in which Internet entry is permissible. Employees of Torstar Corp., their affiliates, agents and members of their immediate families are not eligible. Taxes on the prizes are the sole responsibility of winners. Entry and acceptance of any prize offered constitutes permission to use winner's name, photograph or other likeness for the purposes of advertising, trade and promotion on behalf of Torstar Corp. without further compensation to the winner, unless prohibited by law. Torstar Corp and D.L. Blair, Inc., their parents, affiliates and subsidiaries, are not responsible for errors in printing or electronic presentation of contest or entries. In the event of printing or other errors which may result in unintended prize values or duplication of prizes, all affected contest materials or entries shall be null and void. If for any reason the Internet portion of the contest is not capable of running as planned, including infection by computer virus, bugs, tampering, unauthorized intervention, fraud, technical failures, or any other causes beyond the control of Torstar Corp. which corrupt or affect the administration, secrecy, fairness, integrity or proper conduct of the contest, Torstar Corp. reserves the right, at its sole discretion, to disqualify any individual who tampers with the entry process and to cancel, terminate, modify or suspend the contest or the Internet portion thereof. In the event of a dispute regarding an on-line entry, the entry will be deemed submitted by the authorized holder of the e-mail account submitted at the time of entry. Authorized account holder is defined as the natural person who is assigned to an e-mail address by an Internet access provider, on-line service provider or other organization that is responsible for arranging e-mail address for the domain associated with the submitted e-mail address.

5. Prizes: Grand Prize—a $10,000 vacation to anywhere in the world. Travelers (at least one must be 18 years of age or older) or parent or guardian if one traveler is a minor, must sign and return a Release of Liability prior to departure. Travel must be completed by December 31, 2001, and is subject to space and accommodations availability. Two hundred (200) Second Prizes—a two-book limited edition autographed collector set from one of the Silhouette Anniversary authors: Nora Roberts, Diana Palmer, Linda Howard or Annette Broadrick (value $10.00 each set). All prizes are valued in U.S. dollars.

6. For a list of winners (available after 10/31/00), send a self-addressed, stamped envelope to: Harlequin Silhouette 20th Anniversary Winners, P.O. Box 4200, Blair, NE 68009-4200.

Contest sponsored by Torstar Corp., P.O. Box 9042, Buffalo, NY 14269-9042.

ENTER FOR
A CHANCE TO WIN*

Silhouette's 20th Anniversary Contest

Tell Us Where in the World
You Would Like *Your* Love To Come Alive...
And We'll Send the Lucky Winner There!

Silhouette wants to take you wherever
your happy ending can come true.

Here's how to enter: Tell us, in 100 words or less,
where you want to go to make your love come alive!

In addition to the grand prize, there will be 200
runner-up prizes, collector's-edition book sets
autographed by one of the Silhouette anniversary
authors: **Nora Roberts, Diana Palmer,
Linda Howard** or **Annette Broadrick**.

DON'T MISS YOUR CHANCE TO WIN!
ENTER NOW! No Purchase Necessary

Silhouette®

Where love comes alive™

Visit Silhouette at www.eHarlequin.com to enter, starting this summer.

Name:

Address:

City: State/Province:

Zip/Postal Code:

Mail to Harlequin Books: **In the U.S.**: P.O. Box 9069, Buffalo, NY
14269-9069; **In Canada**: P.O. Box 637, Fort Erie, Ontario, L4A 5X3

*No purchase necessary—for contest details send a self-addressed stamped envelope to:
Silhouette's 20th Anniversary Contest, P.O. Box 9069, Buffalo, NY, 14269-9069 (include
contest name on self-addressed envelope). Residents of Washington and Vermont may
omit postage. Open to Cdn. (excluding Quebec) and U.S. residents who are 18 or over.
Void where prohibited. Contest ends August 31, 2000.   PS20CON_R2